MASTER OF THE HUNT

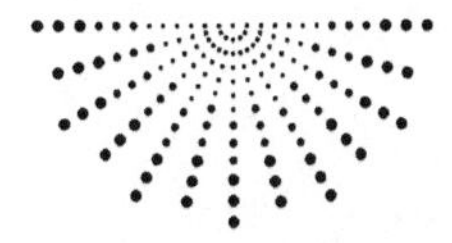

LISA BLACKWOOD

MASTER OF THE HUNT

HUNTRESS VS. HUNTSMAN
BOOK 1

LISA BLACKWOOD

Master of the Hunt
Huntress vs Huntsman: Book 1

Book cover artwork by Ruxandra Tudorica | Methyss Art

www.methyss-art.com

PAPERBACK ISBN: 978-1-990608-12-4

Version 10.16.21

❀ Created with Vellum

BLURB

In a land of three warring kingdoms, a centaur huntsman and a warrior priestess might be the only hope for peace. If the two enemies don't kill each other first, they might even find love.

Seira of Blackstone has fought in many border skirmishes against the centaurs of the lowlands, but when she comes upon a massacre, it's soon apparent the centaur and human dead weren't fighting each other. They were fighting together against a third, unknown foe.

Toryn, a centaur huntsman, is following the trail of a group of soul-mages when he encounters Seira, the most exquisite female he's ever beheld. She's majestic, battle-hardened, strong-willed, and her sharp tongue fires his blood more than any other female he's ever met.

While Seira's natural instinct is to kill the horseman, she's also swift to see they have a better chance of success if they work together.

But there is more danger than just an unknown enemy. As they come to depend on each other, Seira secretly admits she has growing feelings for her centaur partner.

That's a problem.

As a warrior-priestess of the Moon Goddess, Seira has sworn vows of obedience, loyalty, and chastity in exchange for her magic. As such, her body, heart, and soul can never be shared with another. Not even a noble centaur with equal parts desire and tender longing in his eyes.

But centaurs are renowned for their stubborn natures, and Toryn plans to claim Seira's heart even if he risks having the warrior-priestess bury one of her blades in his chest for his troubles.

Author's Note: The Huntress vs Huntsman world is a series of fantasy romance novellas.

Huntress vs Huntsman Reading Order:

Master of the Hunt
Night Huntress
Dragon Archer
Soul Mage

FREE BOOKS

GET TWO FREE STORIES FROM MY BESTSELLING SERIES WHEN YOU SIGN UP FOR MY NEWSLETTER.

I send regular monthly newsletters with details about new releases,
special offers, freebies, and other bookish news.
If that's something you'd be interested in, just follow the link below.

http://lisablackwood.com/join-the-newsletter-here/

CHAPTER ONE

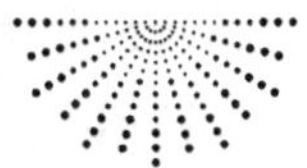

Seira

The river flowed high and fast from recent rains. At last, the sun was out, the day warm and promising to help dry the saturated ground. It had been a wet fall, which made hiding her tracks and the location of her camps more difficult than usual.

Of course, the same conditions had been making it just as difficult for her rival across the river. She grinned suddenly, a rare spark of mirth threading its way through her.

Finding the location of his new camp today had almost made all the rain worthwhile.

Tomorrow, when he headed out for his daily patrol, she'd sneak back across the river and steal something else from his camp. The last time she'd found it two moon cycles ago, she'd stolen his bloody big bow.

It was so large and required such strength, it took everything she had to draw it. But she soothed her pride knowing that she could even without a centaur's size or musculature.

Gazing back across the river, she decided this time she'd steal something more useful than a bloody big bow. She'd always admired his battle-ax. It had a deadly kind of grace to it, and she'd seen him use it enough times—sometimes even against her—that she knew he was proficient with the weapon and would miss it greatly.

Besides, she'd always been curious about the designs she'd seen at a distance. The few times she'd seen it up close, the etchings were nothing more than a blur as she deflected a blow.

Another grin was just spreading across her lips when the sound of an arrow parting the air currents reached her ears. The shaft hissed past her nose a moment before it embedded itself in a tree trunk to her left.

If her pace had been just a bit quicker, she would have stepped right into the line of the arrow's trajectory.

Her gaze locked on the quivering shaft. She recognized it—one she'd made herself only this morning.

Eyes narrowing, she turned and fearlessly glared across the river. Her rival was an excellent shot. If he'd wanted her dead, she'd be dead now.

But even though they were enemies from two sides of a very old conflict, she didn't fear he'd kill her. After all, he'd made it clear by his actions over the years that his life would be much too dull without her.

Reaching blindly, she curled her fingers around the gently quivering arrow, then she snatched it out of the tree and inserted it in her quiver in one smooth, unhurried move.

That she was putting one of her own arrows in her quiver could only mean the industrious centaur had already found her new campsite and had stolen back his favorite bow.

She scanned the opposite bank for him, but he wasn't yet ready to show himself. Wise. She might use the same arrow to put a hole in his pristine palomino hide. Not that she really wanted to harm him. But sometimes he just needed a little warning to put his arrogance in its place.

She'd been sure she'd managed to hide her comings and goings even with the rains. Goddess above! Hadn't she spent more time in the trees than she had on the ground?

And for what?

To have her camp invaded by that horse's ass from across the river?

She grunted her displeasure.

It wasn't the first or even the hundredth time that there had been such an altercation. There had been many such run-ins in the past.

It had started seven years ago when the old centaur huntsman had not returned to take up his post after a long winter. His replacement was the young palomino. And shortly after sizing each other up, she and the new centaur had both decided the other was a prime specimen of the opposite sex, worthy of starting the next generation.

Her reasoning back then wasn't utterly foolish. The centaur huntsman from across the river was a virile looking specimen. And even seven years ago the matrons of Seira's home fortress of Blackstone had been hinting that it would soon be time for her to surrender her territory and the duty of guarding this section of the border to another, younger woman and begin the journey of motherhood.

But that required a male.

And males had been in short supply since the time of

Seira's great, great, great grandmother when the soul-mages had created and released a plague upon the five kingdoms. In a span of seasons, that plague had decimated the male population of Seira's people. The centaurs were not unscathed either, having lost many of their females.

To the best of her knowledge, no kingdom was spared by the plague. The losses were terrible.

But the priestesses of the mountains were not willing to allow the soul-mages the opportunity to enjoy their victory. Seira's ancestors went to the other races and forged alliances where before there had been only rivalry and distrust. Then with the help of the newly allied kingdoms, they defeated the soul-mages.

Unfortunately, the population imbalance created by the mage's plague wasn't so easily defeated.

Yet the matrons of that era had discovered their new centaur allies were capable of shapeshifting into human-looking forms. After peace was restored, the matrons soon set out to discover if a centaur was capable of siring a child on a human woman.

They were. So too were a few of the other races. But the centaurs were the next closest kingdom.

In the first year after the soul-mage plague, the new alliances looked like they might survive and benefit all five kingdoms, but old rivalries soon stressed the treaties, and when sufficient numbers of the opposite sex couldn't be gained by diplomatic means, the most desperate among the various kingdoms turned to less honorable ways.

Widescale raiding exploded along the borders, and soon larger, bloodier wars threatened to break out. Yet the memory of the plague, and how the soul-mages rose to power while the other kingdoms fought amongst themselves, was still fresh in the minds of the victims.

Knowing war would destroy them, the centaurs and the priestesses of the mountains both withdrew deeper into their own lands and eyed each other balefully from afar.

After that, there was no more war, but there wasn't true peace either. Both sides knew they needed members of the opposite gender to continue to procreate, or both species would fade and vanish.

But neither species was willing to become subservient to the other. And the newborn trust that had been gained during the short war with the soul-mages failed to bridge the divide between Seira's ancestors and the centaurs of the lowlands.

Peace and diplomacy ultimately failed a second time, and all five kingdoms prayed to their gods for guidance.

And the gods answered.

It seemed there was one way to stave off extinction.

Bloodless raids.

As strange as it might seem, ritual raids soon became a way of life. Once a year, at the end of the warm season, parties of hunters would venture into enemy territory and attempt to capture prime specimens in their peak breeding years.

Thus, the season of ritualized raiding began, honed over the next two hundred and fifty years as the priestesses learned more about their opponents' way of life.

And seven years ago, Seira had embarked on her first unofficial raid. It had been a disaster from the moment she engaged the palomino centaur in battle.

The ensuing three-day skirmish had nearly given them both heart failure as they tried to overcome and capture their opponent, but they were perfectly matched, two opposing forces, neither willing to surrender or admit defeat. In the end, it turned out to be impossible to take the other alive.

And neither of them had wanted to kill their opponent.

Stalemated, they concluded they were too evenly matched to capture the other without the aid of a hunting party.

And needing someone else to help take down the arrogant centaur lacked the appeal of capturing him all by herself.

"Now who's arrogant?" she asked herself with a little chuckle.

From that day, mutual admiration had grown for the other's tracking and battle skills. Though they were still enemies.

Seira grudgingly admitted the few glimpses she got of the centaur across the river made her daily patrols more interesting. And over the years, catching glimpses of him, or better yet, finding where he'd set up camp, had become a game.

The most recent version of the 'game' was likely the reason she'd just had to pull one of her own arrows out of a tree.

As things do, their game had escalated over the years. At first, it was merely things like sneaking into the other's camp and stealing their evening meal. Soon a simple meal turned into filching arrows and daggers and bows.

Just then, movement on the opposite shore snapped her out of her thoughts. She homed in on that slight flash of color. A moment later, her centaur rival pranced out of the trees and into the shallows.

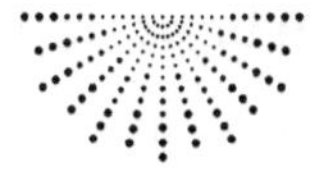

CHAPTER TWO

Seira

She could see his grin from across the river. Presently, he wasn't doing anything more dangerous than enthusiastically waving a large bow above his head as he shouted something at her. Likely an insult, but the roar of the rapids in this section of the river drowned out his words. She could guess them well enough anyway.

When he was done saying his piece, he saluted her.

Her eyes narrowed upon the length of cloth tied around one of his biceps.

"That looks suspiciously like one of my breast

bands," she growled. Her grimace in place, she saluted him in return, flicking her fingers insultingly back at him. "And next time I find your camp, I'm going to steal that bloody damned favorite ax of yours and geld you with it!"

She stormed back to her camp without attempting to hide her trail. There was no point now, anyway. He already knew her camp's location.

Five strides into her well laid out camp, and she knew he'd been busy. There was one deer already dressed, waiting for her. What looked like a second deer's worth of meat hung from her smoking racks.

"Cocky bastard. Probably hunted in my territory, too."

This was just another of their games that had developed over the last two years. She was as guilty as him of crossing the border and hunting in enemy territory, only to later leave her kill in his camp as an insult, saying in a wordless manner that she didn't want to see him return to his herd empty-handed.

After all, it would be a great shame if some of his herd mates starved before spring, thus reducing the pool her people would have to pick from at the end of the next warm season.

However, it was much less fun when he was the one to have found her camp and messed with her things.

From past experiences, she knew she'd now be missing some items. She might not even know what they were right away, not missing them until she needed them.

With a huff, she decided she needed a better way to hide her camp from the relentless centaur huntsman.

One thing was certain—and it hurt her pride to admit it—the centaur was the better tracker.

Grumbling, she stomped toward her tent. After tossing aside the flap, she immediately spotted all her clothing and personal items pulled from their bags and scattered around the floor.

"Bold bastard!" A quick inventory showed that one of her breast bands was missing. A bit more hunting revealed one of her loincloths gone as well.

"That perverted horse's ass. I really am going to steal his damned ax next time."

With jerking motions, she hastily shoved her items back in their proper bags. She was just tying one shut when her gaze landed on the rolled blanket that acted as her pillow.

Two cloth-wrapped bundles rested on it. With a huff, she tossed aside her pack and crawled across her sleeping pallet. She unwrapped the first bundle, which turned out to be one of her stolen breast bands from the last time he'd found her camp a couple months back.

His rich, male scent tickled her nose, and she resisted

the urge to bring it up to her face for a better whiff of the divine scent. She didn't know what it was about centaurs, but whatever pheromone the beasts gave off was nearly addictive.

She continued to unwrap his gift. A wooden carving fell into her hand. It was the figure of a broad-shouldered centaur. Perhaps it was even supposed to be a likeness of her rival?

She studied it with a critical eye.

No.

This beast was heavier set with a more robust frame.

The centaur from across the river was slimmer in build. Still muscular but with a trim and sleek form that better suited a swift huntsman.

Her centaur could no doubt run circles around a beast built like this sculpture.

Her centaur?

Oh, Great Moon Goddess! What mischievous demon had planted that thought in her head?

Giving herself a shake, she pushed aside the disturbing thought and brought the statue closer to her face to study its excellent craftmanship in the dim light inside the tent. She admired the human upper body. It really was very lifelike. She stroked a finger along one high cheekbone and then across the broad brow before continuing down the opposite cheek, following the slope to a strong, square jaw.

The carving's chest was just as muscled as a real centaur. Grinning, she flicked a thumb across the flat male nipples, marveling at the minute details.

Turning the sculpture in her hands, she began to study the horse-like body.

Wait? There was something…

Turning her hand, she tilted the sculpture until the belly was backlit by the open tent flap.

A startled laugh escaped her before she could prevent it. Not stopping to think, she moved her thumb to stroke down the length of the wooden centaur's engorged cock.

Her lips twisting into a grimace, she found herself wondering if centaurs were equally as well-endowed in their human forms.

"Stop that," she scolded herself. "That's exactly what he wants you to be thinking about. Randy beast."

She set aside the statue and looked down at the other cloth-wrapped bundle. After hesitating a moment, she reached forward and swiftly unwrapped a second statue. This one was female and human.

Grunting, she turned it over. The workmanship was just as stunning as the first piece. She eyed the female sculpture with suspicion. If the figure didn't have such wide hips and large breasts, Seira might have thought this statue was depicting her, and that the erotic centaur sculpture was supposed to be her rival from across the river.

"Well. He can just rethink that." She snatched up both figurines and marched from her tent. "Besides, I can always use more kindling."

When she reached her small cooking fire, she noticed it had been built up some time ago and was now nearly ready to begin cooking. She quickly spotted meat already prepared and threaded onto small, bark stripped twigs, just waiting to be cooked.

"Centaur, you're mistaken if you think I can't provide for myself."

Her gaze was just traveling across her camp in the direction of the river to bestow a death-glower in his direction when something white fluttered in the breeze and caught her attention.

A small scrap of parchment sat on a flat rock next to the fire, one corner weighed down by a round river rock.

She circled the fire and then dislodged the rock. Unfolding the valuable bit of paper, she scanned the writing. She'd expected some hard to read scrawl but was surprised.

The male's writing was legible, almost pretty actually. More surprising, the message was written in her own language. At first, she was strangely pleased he'd gone to the trouble of learning her language. Then it occurred to her that the only way he would know her language at all was if he'd forced one of her captive mountain sisters to teach him.

She grimaced but forced herself to calmly read the contents of the note. After all, it could provide valuable insight into this male's mind. While they'd seen each other many times over the years and hurtled numerous insults back and forth, this was the first time he'd written her a note.

Beautiful warrior,

I know you have no reason to trust me beyond the few dealings we have had with each other, but I feel it is only honorable to warn you that one of my peoples' raiding parties is due to journey through my assigned territory tomorrow.

Shield your camp well and hide any of your footpaths. I have already covered the ones I found.

. . .

May the Lord of the Forests and the Lady of the Prairies shelter and protect you.

Your companion and rival,
  Toryn of the wildland prairie.

Seira read the note a second time and still found herself surprised by the words.

He was warning her. Why?

That came as a surprise. But the more she thought about it, the more she came to understand what might be his driving reason for warning her.

He didn't want her caught by other males.

Not that she would ever allow a male to gain the upper hand long enough to catch her.

But that didn't mean her rival might not still have designs on her as his own mate.

The thought didn't concern her long. She snorted in humor. If he ever attempted to make any amorous attentions known, she'd put him in his place.

But that didn't mean his words of warning weren't valid and shouldn't be heeded.

And even if they were lies, she would still heed them.

It was better to be prepared for an attack that would never come than to be caught unawares.

It certainly wouldn't do her any harm to hide anything that might lead a hunting party to her camp. Then she'd keep an eye out to see if Toryn betrayed her by leading the other centaurs to her location.

Her eyes settled on the wooden figurines again.

Now that she knew they were depictions of his two deities, they seemed not quite as vulgar or suggestive as she'd first assumed. Her gaze slid to the centaur carving, and her lips twisted into a grin as she gazed at its erect not-so-little phallus.

She changed her mind. It was still vulgar in nature, but her studies had told her enough about her enemies to know their father god—the Lord of the Forest—was often portrayed as strong and virile, with one of his powers being the ability to bless and make barren wombs fertile once more.

The Lady of the Prairies shared a similar nature, which would explain the carving's thick hips and heavy breasts.

After reading Toryn's note, she was sure her centaur rival really was trying to invoke his gods' protection on her behalf.

It would have been sweet if he hadn't also been one of her enemies, and a long-standing thorn in her side.

Perhaps it was time to visit him to see if he'd been truthful about what he'd said.

Besides, it would be beneficial to know the whereabouts of the centaur hunting party, so the one led by her younger sisters due to arrive shortly didn't accidentally run into the enemy hunt.

Grinning, Seira decided even if there hadn't been two different hunting parties in play, it was still past time she paid her rival another visit. She'd been admiring that ax of his for quite some time.

CHAPTER THREE

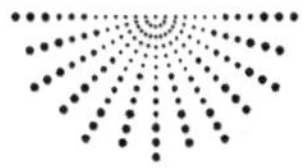

Seira

After Seira crossed the river, she took to the trees and did a thorough search of the land surrounding Toryn's camp. The last thing she needed was the hunting party mentioned in his letter to find her snooping through his camp. But her search turned up nothing.

Calling on her stealth magic, she slowly lowered herself to the ground. Crouching, she surveyed his camp for a moment more. Then after making sure her stealth magic was reflecting her surroundings in perfect mimicry, she continued deeper into his camp.

After a quick scan of the area, she tucked her own note under a rock next to his fire. If she'd had time, she would have hunted and left a kill for him to even the score, but she might not have time.

As it was, the sun was low in the sky, long shadows stretching across the ground around her. Toryn would be returning any time now.

Hurrying through his camp, she searched for his great war ax, but it wasn't anywhere. She'd found his sword in his tent and had been tempted to steal that, but it didn't draw her as much as the ax.

Even though he had his longbow, he'd likely kept the ax on his person so she couldn't steal it.

"Overly vigilant centaur," she muttered under her breath.

The ax was the only thing of value she hadn't been able to steal over the years. She needed to get her hands on that ax. It was a point of pride. A way of restoring her honor.

In the years she'd known him, he'd managed to steal just about everything she owned twice. It didn't matter that he'd always eventually returned everything. She needed that ax to even the score. And she would return it to him—in time—once she'd had time to gloat at him from across the river.

The distant sounds of a single set of hoofbeats

announced the return of the centaur. Turning, she hurried over to a tree at the edge of his camp.

After quickly climbing halfway up, she settled in to wait. She'd never before tested her stealth magic while perched in a tree at the edge of her rival's camp, but she'd gotten close to him in the past, and he'd never found her hiding spot when her magic was strong. And right at this moment her magic was at its peak, the Maiden's Moon high in the sky, feeding her strength. Of the Moon Goddess's three moons, it was the greatest in power.

She couldn't say what mischievous spirit had infected her and made her stay behind for a bird's eye view of the centaur's response to her invasion of his territory. But she sat and grinned and waited for his arrival.

The wait wasn't long.

Toryn trotted into his camp and looked around, his sharp eyes already spotting the faint tracks and traces she'd left and hadn't bothered to disguise.

She wanted him to know she'd been all over his camp, touching all his things, deciding what she'd steal.

Below her, he started unbuckling the harness that held a large elk on his back. He gave a few expert tugs and swiftly dropped his kill on the ground. It had already been dressed, she noted. But she had little interest in the deer.

He paused under her tree. With a grin, she took the opportunity to study him.

A thick mop of dark black hair with light brown highlights was tied back at the base of his neck, but some of his mane still managed to flow across his shoulders and down his back in thick waves.

Sweat gleamed on his human shoulders, catching her attention and drawing her gaze to them. They were just as wide and well-muscled as she remembered. A powerful chest angled into a sturdy waist. Where a human male's flanks would have flared out into hips, Toryn's merged seamlessly with his equine shoulders and withers. Skin of a deep tan merged into a golden palomino coat shaded darker by the sweat of his exertions.

The evidence of his hard work didn't distract from his magnificence, she noted. It added to it.

From this angle, she was able to get a good look at the darker dorsal strip that ran from where his human lower back merged with his equine withers. The mark ran the length of his spine to the tip of his tail. Even there, the dark swatch of hair blended naturally with the more substantial portion of blond in his tail.

Her gaze trailed along his form, watching as his

powerful muscles flexed and flowed under silky hide and skin alike. He really was splendid to behold.

All centaurs were. They blended human and horse traits into a strange and beautiful medley of the wild and the domesticated.

Seira fought the urge to drop down on his equine back and find out if his gaits would feel like a regular horse. Such a notion was entirely foolish, and she swiftly crushed that desire. Instead, she held her place. Getting bucked off a centaur wasn't on today's list of misadventures.

Below her, Toryn studied his camp, his head turning as he followed her near-invisible trail. His gaze paused at the fire ring and the note she'd left for him there.

With an eager spin of his tail, he trotted over to it. Seira noted the extra spring in his step. He was almost prancing in his excitement.

As she grinned down at him, she began to realize his task was likely just as lonely as hers. Whatever the cause, he was swift to reach down and snatch up her letter. He read it rapidly.

With his back to her, she couldn't see his face, but she could see his shoulders start to shake a moment before his rich, deep laughter filled the clearing.

Still chuckling, he continued around the camp, touching some of the same items she had.

She marveled at his ability to track her movements so precisely. Slowly it crept into her consciousness that hiding in a tree at the edge of his camp likely wasn't one of her brighter ideas. Yet they'd been playing this particular game so long, she didn't really feel threatened by him.

But he never came back to her tree. Instead, he started discarding his gear as he trotted toward the river. Unfortunately, he kept his ax with him.

Considering the amount of sweat covering him, she'd bet he was headed to the river for a bath. If that was the case, she might still have a chance to nab his ax.

"The damn centaur better not bathe with his ax," she muttered.

Once the sound of his steps faded, she eased down the side of the tree. Leaving the camp behind, she skirted wide of the path he'd taken.

She followed the river, approaching him downwind, her steps soft and cautious. One misplaced step, a snapped twig, a displaced pebble—any one of those mishaps would be enough to give away her location to the sharp-eared centaur.

But as she drew closer, the splash of water reached her. And in this section of the river, there were no rapids, the river calm and mirror-like. The occasional splash could only be the centaur.

Another grin spread across her face.

He was already in the river. Stealing the ax would be as easy as darting in while his back was turned and taking the weapon. She could be in and out before he even knew his ax was gone.

Of course, she'd have to be swift to reach the tree line and scramble back up into the canopy before he could run her down. She was no match for a centaur on the ground.

But in the trees?

In the trees, she was mistress.

CHAPTER FOUR

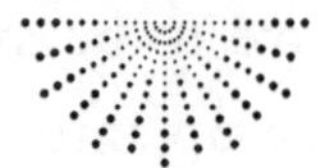

Seira

As soon as she reached the place where he'd entered the river, Seira's plan encountered a hitch. There was precious little cover. Which wouldn't have been a big problem with her stealth magic helping to hide her. But unfortunately, the big centaur was already walking toward shore.

She bit back the urge to curse creatively. Her magic didn't hide sound. The last thing she needed was to be caught out here in the open. Hunching lower in the tall grass, she started to backtrack.

As she turned her full attention upon the centaur

huntsman, her breath caught.

He was walking up the sandy bank. As he emerged from the water, she noticed he wasn't in his horse form. He'd shifted to the form of a man. She knew all centaurs possessed the ability, but she'd never seen his human body up close before.

Her gaze darted over his naked form before she could stop herself. His lower half was just as toned and muscled and golden as his upper half. Then she allowed her curious gaze to rove over the smooth expanse of his muscular flanks.

He was already past her position, so she couldn't see what he looked like from the front—something she shouldn't be interested in anyway, she reminded herself. But the view from behind was surprisingly lovely. She watched the firm, lean globes of his ass until the tall grasses obscured the view.

Goddess! He was magnificent. Did all men used to look like that?

Perhaps if the matrons had offered her a male like Toryn, she might not have turned down their offer to become one of the Mothers. Or at least, she might have paused and thought about it for a while before rejecting their offer.

But Seira loved her duty as one of her queendom's guards. In the end, she doubted any male could make her choose him over the life she loved out here in the wilderness.

That didn't mean she couldn't still enjoy the momentary distraction Toryn offered. Realizing her thoughts had tilted toward blasphemy, she glanced up at the sky, her gaze finding the maiden's moon. The two other sister moons were not yet in the sky, but as long as even one rode the vast blue expanse, it was said their goddess could hear them easily.

"Forgive me for my momentary distraction. I won't allow it to happen often. Certainly not enough to jeopardize my honor or my duty to you, Great Mother."

While she'd been reassuring herself, Toryn had continued to where he'd left a pack. Hunching, he reached down and unbuckled one of his pack's straps. After rummaging around inside the pack for a moment, he pulled out a thick blanket and unfolded it on the ground.

While he was busy, she moved closer and watched as he used one bare foot to flick back an errant corner of the blanket before he laid down.

What was he doing?

Resting?

Napping?

Air drying?

Whatever the case might be, this new development

was her second chance at his ax.

Decision made—foolish or not—she eased her way closer to his position, being careful not to so much as stir a blade of grass.

When she reached his location, she found him stretched out on the blanket, his hands folded behind his head, utterly relaxed.

He was sunning himself in the last of the day's light, she realized with a little envy.

With his eyes closed, he looked wholly peaceful.

She would have suspected a trap, except he was absolutely defenseless at the moment. His ax was out of reach, and he had no other weapons with him. He didn't even have his centaur speed and strength to call upon in his present form.

She studied his face for a moment more and then decided he wasn't faking his relaxation. He really was sunning himself. Running her palms against her knees in a distracted manner, she allowed her gaze to wander south of his navel.

The muscles of his lower abdomen formed a sort of wedge that directed her eyes downward. There was a delicate tracery of darker blond hair that started just below his navel and grew somewhat thicker at his groin.

He wasn't overly hairy there, just enough to draw her eyes to the length of his manhood. Even at rest, it looked impressive. At least she thought it did. She didn't have anything to compare it to except the statues and paintings back at the fortress.

It was wrong to stay and stare. She was here for the ax, she reminded herself. The ax was just out of reach from her present position.

But if she skirted to his other side, she could quickly snatch up the ax and retreat the way she'd come. She just had to wait until he was asleep.

Any guilt she might have felt was assuaged by the knowledge he'd probably spied upon her at some point over the years. Or he would have if he ever managed to get close enough without her knowing.

And now he was here, sleeping, completely unaware she was within touching distance.

Her gaze tracked back to the ax. That great big ax of his was still calling her name. She was so close; she could almost feel the handle in her hand.

And the arrogant male had fallen asleep without putting up any magical protection. He was practically begging to be robbed of his valuables.

Then the decision made, she moved from her crouch among the tall grasses. She paused every few steps to be sure nothing gave away her presence.

She was almost within striking distance when a

sharp bark of laughter startled her so badly, she nearly leaped out of her skin.

Her training didn't fail her, though. She slammed one hand into his opposite shoulder to keep him down while her other hand pressed the edge of a long dagger against his throat.

"I didn't actually think you'd come this close." Toryn's rich voice wrapped around her. The hint of humor in his tone was unmistakable.

"You underestimated my desire for your ax."

He looked up at her, his expression and body language relaxed, as if having a warrior-priestess hold a knife to his throat was an everyday occurrence. But he wasn't completely unaffected. His eyes, usually a beautiful silver-blue, had darkened to a stormier color.

"Are you sure it is only my ax you covet, Priestess?" A cocky little smile touched his lips.

She pressed the edge of her blade harder against his throat until a small bead of blood welled up.

He didn't so much as blink or look away from her intense gaze.

Now, now. She couldn't have him being all confident and assured, not when he was naked and had an equally naked blade pressed to his throat.

Smiling coldly, she drew a second dagger and straddled him. Then leaning forward, she purred in his ear, "What else would I want from a centaur?"

"I can think of a few things." His lips turned up, his humor growing.

Insufferable male pretending he wasn't afraid even when she knew he had to be feeling mighty vulnerable. Perhaps it was time to make him feel even more helpless.

"Are you offering me something besides your great big ax? Should I finish what we started seven years ago and tie you up and take you home and present you to my House at last?" She settled a bit more heavily on him and rocked suggestively.

She knew he didn't want to become a slave any more than she did. And he was likely regretting taking on his more vulnerable human form right about now. But her attempt to call his bluff didn't quite work out as she'd planned.

His eyes darkened further as a slight pink flush crawled across his high cheekbones. Naked and pinned under her, there was no way for him to hide his response to her. She felt as his manhood reacted, growing hard and eager to serve. A moment later, his hips shifted, and his eyes closed, head tilting back as if inviting her to nip his throat with her lips and teeth instead of her blade.

She dipped lower and inhaled his scent deep into her lungs. It truly was the most divine of smells. Exhaling against his neck, she almost hummed in pleasure.

Toryn's lips parted on a groan.

Goddess! The carnal creature was actually enjoying being pinned by her while she threatened him with her blades. Her attempt to inspire fear had failed miserably, but she couldn't let him know that. And she certainly wouldn't let him know how much his evident desire unsettled her.

He shifted again, jerking up against the seam of her pants before he mastered himself. She thought it may have been involuntary by the darker flush of red that washed across his cheeks.

"Behave yourself, Horseman. It would be a shame if I had to geld such a lovely specimen. And then the matrons would certainly weep at the loss of such a virile creature."

She should have been bolting away from him, but she found herself looking down at him and marveling at his masculine beauty instead. Even after seven years, his features still had a hint of the boyish charm he'd had all those seasons ago when she'd first spied upon him.

He'd grown no less handsome as he'd matured, she admitted. Though his firm lips were still quick to show humor, and if she wasn't mistaken, his eyes still held a kindness and gentleness from an earlier time in his life. He wasn't yet jaded.

"Horseman, your eyes give too much away. As does your face. Any fool could see how trusting you really are. I'm surprised you've lived this long."

And her words were true.

While he was skilled in weapons and the best tracker she'd ever crossed, he lacked the harsh relentlessness she'd seen in other huntsmen over the years.

She found that fascinating. And fascination was something too dangerous for a warrior-priestess to feel.

"Perhaps I only show that vulnerability to a person I know I can trust," Toryn said, his deep voice wrapping around her. "To address your earlier comment, while I will admit interest in what could be shared between us, I have no wish to be a slave to a woman of the mountains. Not even one as lovely as you."

"Hmmm." She leaned forward until her lips were touching one of his softly furred and pointed ears. It flicked and twitched before flattening against his head, attempting to vanish into his thick hair. How adorable. "That's regrettable about not wanting to be a slave."

"Yes. But I like our games a great deal," he added. "What if we came to another arrangement?"

"Another arrangement?"

"We can continue as we have been, but with a few more benefits."

Seira decided she loved the sound of his voice. She didn't really care what he said; she just loved listening to his rich tones and lilting accent.

And that was also too dangerous.

"Or I could just steal your ax." She leaped away from him and snatched up his weapon.

Before he'd even sat up, she was racing away with her prize gripped in her hand.

His laughter gave chase. "If you ever change your mind, you know where to find me."

Grinning, she hefted the ax higher as she ran. Yes, she knew where to find him.

She planned to always know where to find her rival.

CHAPTER FIVE

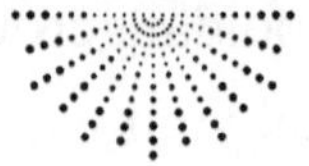

Seira

The next morning Seira was still unsettled by events from the day before. Toryn had even haunted her dreams, the insufferable male. Feeling groggy and out of sorts, she forced herself up early to do a patrol of her territory.

Just because she was tired didn't mean threats wouldn't visit her land. And if Toryn hadn't been lying, a party of centaurs was likely on its way. And Toryn's face was pretty expressive. She doubted he was an accomplished liar.

She kept her senses sharp and searched for any sign

of the rival hunting party. She also looked for signs of one of the Hunts sent out from Blackstone fortress.

Seira's two younger sisters were taking part in this year's Hunts. While she wouldn't betray Toryn's location to even her sisters, she would tell her sisters' Hunt about the rival centaurs.

If Moraja or Brewin were able to call together the other two Hunts, the combined might of the warrior-priestesses would be enough to overpower the armed company of centaurs. The matrons would be well pleased with the great harvest of males. And Toryn would be safe from the Hunt for another year.

Now all Seira had to do was find her sisters' tardy Hunt. She wasn't concerned that they'd run afoul of the rival centaur Hunt. She hadn't heard any sounds of battle.

It was also possible the younger warrior-priestesses were too eager to postpone their hunt by coming to Seira's territory first. They might just have forged ahead, seeking one of the other border guardians for any news of centaur movements.

Seira's family was a tad competitive. She wouldn't put it past her younger siblings to go out and capture themselves a centaur and then brag about it to her later.

Wouldn't they be surprised when she came with news of an entire Hunt of centaurs ripe for the picking.

And if the only way to stop any future gloating was to help capture a few centaurs, then she'd aid her sisters in their hunt.

Under normal circumstances, Seira wouldn't leave her stretch of border unguarded, but the news of a centaur hunting party was of greater importance to her people. Once the centaurs were captured, Seira would return to her own territory and her intriguing rival across the river.

Grinning, she turned back toward her camp to pack some supplies and ready her little mountain horse. The beast wasn't overly fast, but he could move swifter over the rough terrain than she could carrying her supplies.

Once she'd left her territory behind, it hadn't taken Seira long to find the path the mountain women had taken. Their horses' tracks were easy to follow.

It was also as she'd expected. Her sisters or the other members of their hunting party were too excited to take the time to visit Seira. They were taking the most direct route toward centaur territory.

Seira assumed once they were closer, they would disguise their presence as they entered enemy territory.

After all, they were fully trained warrior-priestesses. They hadn't survived this long with lackluster skills.

To judge by the age of the tracks, the hunting party had crossed this ground late yesterday. The larger group wouldn't be able to travel through the dense forest as swiftly as a single horse and rider. Seira judged she would overtake them before noon.

Then she could pass on the information about the rival Hunt and aid in setting an ambush for them. If all went well, she'd be back in her own territory before Toryn could steal any more of her underthings.

With a chuckle, she urged her horse to hurry his slow walk into something that resembled a trot.

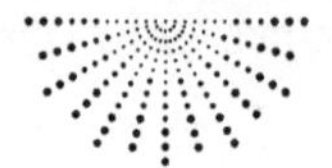

Toryn

Nervous excitement made Toryn's skin twitch. His tail flicked at flies that weren't there as he galloped toward his destination. He'd emerged from his tent just as the dawn pinked the sky, too excited to sleep more. He'd started off, his pace swift and sure. Near boundless energy fueled him from the events of the day before.

She'd finally come to him. He'd talked to her. Learned her name. Seira was a beautiful name. Sure and strong sounding, and yet there was a delicacy to it. Just like the woman.

But as much as he would have liked to sneak across the river to observe her more, he had a duty to his people. After checking his territory, he'd headed out in the direction he knew the company of centaurs would be coming.

He was to meet them and act as a guide, helping them locate the other mountain women that guarded the border. And in the process, he would lead them away from Seira. He could do that much to keep her safe, at least.

He continued to gallop tirelessly for half the morning, his mind on Seira.

It wasn't until he turned down one of the main game trails that his keen sense of smell picked up the scent of many strangers. He slowed and began scanning the area. He soon found where the large company of riders had emerged from the denser forest onto the game trail.

They were riding mountain horses by the size of the hoofprints, which could only mean these were warrior-priestesses. It was likely the Hunt Seira's letter had warned him about.

And to his delight, they were headed in the same direction he was, toward the centaur company. Perhaps he wouldn't have to be away from his territory and the lovely Seira as long as he'd thought. If he could find the centaur hunters and help them set an ambush, he need not be away the entire month.

Grinning, tail whipping behind him, he kicked out his heels and gave chase.

Once he was close enough to confirm their number and armaments, he'd cut out around the troop of women and outpace them, and then he'd locate the centaurs. Helping them set an ambush for the women wouldn't be that hard.

As strong as the warrior-priestesses were, he'd only crossed one who was his match, and she was safely behind him.

CHAPTER SEVEN

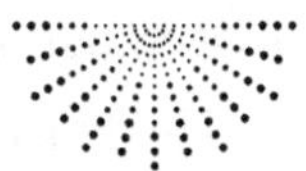

Toryn

As things tended to do when he was in a good mood, Toryn's plan hit a snag. Shortly after he'd started to cut cross-country, he'd found another set of tracks. These belonged to Seira's sturdy little mountain horse. One of gelding's hooves had a slight imperfection, and that was how he knew Seira was somewhere on the trail ahead of him.

Now he had until he met up with the centaur company to think of a plan that would allow Seira to escape the capture of the rest of the mountain women.

To judge by the tracks, she was still a distance behind

the other women. Perhaps there was a way he could waylay her. Though as willing as she was to warn him of the danger, he doubted she'd just stand by and allow her fellow priestesses to be captured.

Still, he'd find a way to protect her even if he had to betray every last scrap of trust he'd been building up with her over the years. He'd do it if it meant keeping her safe. He'd rather feel her hatred than see her freedom curtailed.

But first, he had to catch up.

Cursing, he galloped after her.

Apparently, fate wasn't done with him. As the afternoon stretched longer and he continued his mad gallop, something—an unfamiliar scent—teased at his senses. And not in a good way. This scent held a hint of sickly sweetness. It was almost floral, but not. It was mustier in nature. Something about it reminded him of old death.

A chill crept across his body.

As he galloped full speed toward the unknown danger, his magic continued to awaken and raised more of an alarm. A distant memory stirred.

When he'd still been a colt, he'd much preferred to gallop and spar with others his age, but his father's historian had sometimes managed to pin him down long enough for a few lessons.

One lesson he remembered vividly was of the soul-mages and how they had nearly wiped out his species and the other races. The historian said the soul-mages' magic held a hint of flowery musk and death-scent.

It was said to cling to whatever the mage touched and to linger where a soul-mage had walked. As if their very presence corrupted the ground they trod upon.

And somewhere ahead, Seira was heading straight toward that threat.

CHAPTER EIGHT

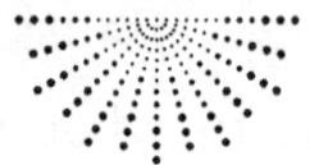

Seira

Even before she found the first body, she knew by the coppery scent of blood and the stench of ruptured bowels it wasn't going to be good. She found a centaur first. He'd been impaled by a spear. The shaft was made of metal, not wood. And when she pulled it from the body for a closer look, she noted the crystal spearhead glowed with an unnatural power. Seira hissed and dropped it on the ground. Even just touching it made her feel unclean.

It wasn't of a design used by either her people or the lowland centaurs. Soon she saw other evidence of battle.

Two mountain women had fallen at the side of another centaur.

Seira wasn't as good at reading tracks as Toryn, so she couldn't say if the centaur had been protecting the women or if it was the other way around, but clearly, they were working together against another enemy. A new enemy both sides must have recognized as a greater threat.

Not able to discover anything else of importance—and not willing to waste time since she didn't know what had attacked and killed these four souls, and also not knowing what her two sisters might even now be facing without her—Seira rushed to her gelding and hurriedly mounted. She urged the beast into a gallop and wished she sat something much fleeter of foot.

CHAPTER NINE

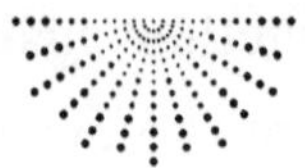

Toryn

The horror he felt at seeing the first bodies was muted by the fear he felt for Seira. As he'd closed the distance between them, he'd been able to see she too had been closing the gap, if more slowly.

He'd never been so thankful for her slow little horse. The beast had likely saved Seira's life. But Toryn wouldn't relax until he knew she was safe.

And at the moment, he didn't know that at all.

Just because her horse was slow and had likely saved her from the same fate suffered by the bodies he'd galloped by, it didn't mean she wouldn't run into trouble if she kept hunting the soul-mages.

To either side of him, the forest thinned, opening into a lush grass-covered valley. He followed a stream down the steep slope. Soon it would be sunset, and he'd lose the light, but as he walked farther out of the forest, his gaze swiftly found the main site of the battle.

The other bodies he'd seen along the trail had been survivors trying to escape, perhaps to warn their people that soul-mages once again walked the land.

A shiver raced down Toryn's sweat-covered body.

His human and equine chests heaved, both sets of lungs working to deliver enough air to his starved muscles.

But he was here.

And he wasn't alone.

Another figure ghosted from body to body down at the valley floor where thick evening mist was already beginning to gather.

His hearts pounded, and his legs nearly shook with relief. He'd know that form anywhere.

Seira.

Seira lived.

He left the stream for the better footing of the grass-covered banks, and then he was galloping toward her.

She looked up and saw his approach, but she didn't call out or respond in any way, merely returning to her diligent search.

While she might be checking for anyone still alive, he didn't think that was it. Her body language was too closed off, as if she was trying to protect herself from some emotional hurt as she searched.

"Oh, my poor priestess," he whispered. "You're seeking the fate of a loved one."

Before he could join her to aid in the search, she froze over a body. A moment later, she dropped to the ground next to it, her shoulders shaking in silent sobs.

He slowed, sensing she needed time to grieve alone. He would give her that time.

Longbow in hand and sword ready at his hip, he guarded his warrior-priestess while she grieved.

CHAPTER TEN

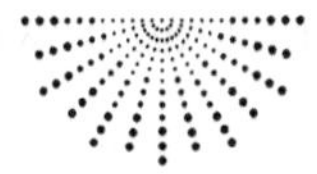

Seira

Rage and grief were at war in her chest, both fighting to escape in anguished screams as she held the bodies of her two younger sisters and rocked them gently. They'd fallen together, centaurs on either side of them.

Seira's one bit of solace was that they hadn't died alone.

But they shouldn't have died at all.

"I should have been here with them."

"If you were, you'd have died."

Toryn. She'd seen the centaur approaching. Knew he

was standing close. Guarding her. But she hadn't been able to bring herself to speak with him earlier.

That had been what? An hour ago? More? Less?

Time seemed to have no meaning. Yet another part of her mind knew it did. The longer she sat here help-less, the farther away the enemy would get.

And that couldn't be allowed to happen.

She needed to pull herself together, needed to hunt down the monsters responsible for this. And she couldn't do it alone. But by the time reinforcements answered her horn's call, the enemy would be too far away to catch.

From what she'd learned before arriving at the battle site, she knew the enemy had horses. Large, fast horses.

She turned toward the centaur. But she still couldn't speak. Couldn't even look up at him. Her throat was too tight with the effort of holding in the rage and anguish.

"Priestess," he said softly.

Her title was almost like an irresistible summons coming from his lips.

She looked back up at him.

"We have a decision to make," he noted.

She squared her shoulders. "There is no decision, Centaur. I'm going after the soul-mages. I don't have a choice. If I don't go after them now, they will ride back to the ocean, and once on a boat, I'll never find them or the souls of my sisters or the rest of my people again."

And it was a fate worse than death for a soul captured by a soul-mage. The mages used the souls to lengthen their own lifespans, absorbing the lifeforce along with the soul's magic and memories.

It was truly an evil unlike anything else Seira could compare it to. It was never-ending slavery where the master stole everything a person had ever been.

"I'll leave as soon as I've blessed the bodies and lit the pyre. There's no time to observe the normal three days of mourning."

"We," the centaur said in his deep tones.

She looked up at him sharply, and he nodded ever so slightly. "We leave as soon as the pyre is lit. The soul-mages killed my people and stole their souls as well. And even if none of my people had been victims, I would go with you. A soul-mage is an atrocity that should not be allowed to exist in the natural world."

He wasn't wrong. And with his tracking skills and her battle magic, they would both stand a better chance of hunting down the enemy together than alone.

Toryn walked a half-circle around her, gazing out at the battlefield. "You can see by the position of the farthest bodies and the other tracks that the priestesses were the first to encounter the mages. Most of them didn't stand a chance. See that scorched earth to the west?"

Seira looked in the direction he pointed and then nodded.

"That was the kill spell. By the damage, it was set to trigger after two-thirds of the priestesses crossed that section of the valley." He paused and looked up at the sky. "I can't be sure of the timing, but I think it was just after the first moon had set and before the second had risen."

"It was timed perfectly when the priestesses would be at their weakest," Seira said, her tone bitter.

"Yes. And unlike a centaur, your people have no way of sensing the soul-mages. They didn't know they were walking into a trap. They didn't have a chance to call on their protective shields." His voice lowered. "The survivors farther back fought but were greatly outnumbered. Though it looks like they killed a number of the soul-mages."

"The centaurs?" Seira asked suddenly. "How were they involved?"

Toryn nodded toward the eastern slope of the valley. "The centaurs either heard the fighting or may have even scented the soul-mages and were tracking them. Whatever alerted them, they came to fight alongside the priestesses."

"And died for their troubles," Seira said, bitterness thick in her voice.

"Yes," he agreed softly. "We are formidable warriors, but our particular variety of magic is little use against a soul-mage's spells."

"Your people were very gallant. They could have simply gone for reinforcements."

Toryn snorted. "A centaur will never leave a female when she's in danger. It doesn't matter the species."

Seira made a gruff sound. "I don't need your protection, Centaur."

"No. But you need my tracking spells, and I need your battle magic."

She looked up sharply.

Toryn arched an eyebrow. "This time it will be the soul-mages caught unawares. We will track them down and then pick them off one by one when they least expect it and steal back each and every one of our peoples' souls."

"Very well, Centaur." Seira inclined her head to him. "We'll walk together until vengeance has been satisfied."

He snorted again, a distinctively horse-like sound of amusement. "I'd prefer to gallop. We won't catch the soul-mages otherwise. There isn't time to rally our peoples and form a large fighting force. By the time our people gather, the soul-mages will have escaped out to sea. Once they hit the ocean, we'll have no way of tracking the enemy."

Seira nodded but noticed there was a problem with his plan.

"My little gelding will not be able to make the journey in the time needed."

"No," Toryn agreed. "But isn't it good you made friends with a centaur?"

Under other circumstances, she was sure there would have been humor in his tone, and she likely would have some biting remark to toss back at him. But just now, surrounded by death, she simply nodded and thanked both their gods for sending Toryn into her life.

CHAPTER ELEVEN

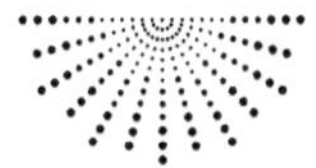

Toryn

Gathering wood to make the pyres and tending to the bodies took until dawn. Toryn could see how hard it was on Seira when it came time to bless the bodies of her younger siblings and allow him to place them on their pyre.

He set them with care at the top, closest to the stars. A place of great honor and respect among his people. Their souls might still be trapped far away, but he hoped the spirits would hear his and Seira's pledges, that neither of them would rest until all the trapped souls were freed to make the journey to the next life.

By mutual agreement, he and Seira agreed to leave the dead of the soul-mages to feed the wildlife. They didn't deserve the honor of prayers and last rites.

As he set the last pyre ablaze, Seira sang to her goddess, asking the Lady of the Moons to comfort and protect the souls of the dead even though they were unable to make the journey. Then once the priestess was finished with her rituals, she began a second, invoking and beseeching the god and goddess of the centaurs to do the same for their faithful.

Toryn was touched by her thoughtfulness.

By the time she was finished, dawn was stretching pink fingers across the sky in the east.

"If you're not too tired, we should go." Her voice was still gruff with pain and anguish, but there was determination there too.

"A centaur is never too tired for vengeance."

CHAPTER TWELVE

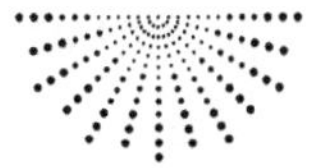

Seira

Her fingers closed over the buckles of Toryn's pack harness as she checked to make sure everything was secure and well balanced one final time. The last thing he needed on a long journey was to get sore from an ill-fitting load.

Speaking of loads. "Are you sure about this? If you carry me, won't the added weight slow you too much? We might be just as far ahead keeping me on my gelding."

He eyed her, taking longer than was likely necessary to judge her weight, but she didn't question him.

"You should see how much I carry when I make the monthly trips back to the huntsmens' camp to deliver the dried meat and hides." He shrugged. "I doubt you even weigh a quarter of that."

She knew from her earlier studies that centaurs were beastly strong; their natural magic giving them superior speed, strength, and stamina that surpassed what a normal horse possessed. If he said he could carry her weight without strain, she believed him.

"Very well. It's your back."

He seemed surprised by the ease with which he'd secured her agreement.

This time it was Seira's turn to grin. "You're very brave to allow an armed enemy on your back."

Her one thumb stroked across the emerald in her sword's hilt.

Toryn laughed openly. "If you were going to kill me, you would have done it long before now. Besides, you had ample opportunity to bury your blade in my chest when I was naked at the river, but you didn't."

"Hmmm. Don't make me regret that."

"I'll never do anything to you that you'll regret." His hand settled on her shoulder. His thumb stroked slowly along her collarbone.

She drew her sword in one swift move, the tip pressing up against his throat in a return caress. To his credit, he didn't pale or flush or even so much as widen his eyes in surprise. Though he held himself perfectly still.

"Centaur, I agree we should partner up. Your stamina, strength, and speed will combine with my battle and stealth magic most elegantly and make for a beneficial partnership. But don't think I'll trade my magic, all that I am, for a moment's pleasure." She paused and gave him a very slight prod with her blade, enough to draw a bead of blood, but he didn't rear back. "But if you press for more in our new partnership, you will find yourself very swiftly a ghost. Do I make myself clear?"

"Exceptionally." His voice was even deeper than usual. And if it was possible, she thought her threat had only succeeded in arousing him more.

She rolled her eyes.

Males!

CHAPTER THIRTEEN

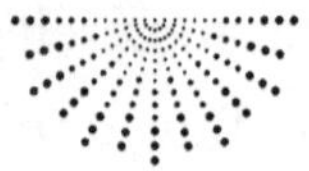

Seira

At last, all the buckles on the harness were adjusted, their combine supplies packed. Now Toryn waited, facing forward. Seira took note of the height of his back. He was a lot taller at the withers than her mountain horse. The centaur made her horse look like a foal in comparison.

Usually she'd grab a fistful of mane, place her other hand on the horse's rump, and then vault up and swing a leg over. But she felt that might be taking liberties with a centaur.

She cleared her throat and then squared her shoulders. When she had a suitably stern expression on her face, she addressed the male. "How is mounting a centaur different than mounting a horse? Do I just leap up and swing a leg over?"

Toryn glanced over his shoulder at her before looking straight ahead again. After a moment, his shoulders began to shake.

"What's so funny?" she snapped. Then she realized what she'd said. "Mounting? Really? If you're going to be that juvenile, I think I should just kill you now and take my chances on my own."

Toryn turned to her and held up his hands. "Sorry. It just struck me as funny. I was wondering how desperate you mountain women—"

"Stop. Talking. Or your new title will be 'the gelding.' Do I make myself clear?"

Toryn made a humorous wheezing snort and danced to the side, putting distance between them, but after a moment, he returned to her side and held out an arm to help her mount.

"Here, brace yourself against my forearm."

She did as he suggested, and when she vaulted up, he helped propel her the rest of the way up onto his back. Shifting forward, she put a little room between her backside and the packs. Of course, that meant she was now nearly brushing up against his human torso with each of his steps.

It also highlighted the fact she didn't know what to do with her hands. Normally, she'd be holding reins, gripping her horse's mane, or holding her saddle if he was lunging up a steep hill. But she had none of those things. There was only a thick blanket between her backside and the centaur's spine. No stirrups. And the centaur's gait was different than a horse's. She wasn't yet secure in her seat.

"What am I supposed to do with my hands?" she muttered in frustration.

Blessedly, Toryn didn't so much as snicker. "Put them around my waist."

She did as he suggested, but somehow the angle was wrong. Finally, she just scooted forward until her front was pressed up against his back. "I've never ridden a centaur before. Tell me if this position is going to hurt you."

"I think it will be fine. Back home many centaurs do carry riders."

"You make it sound like you don't." Seira wondered about that. Was it because he was too proud or didn't like the closeness?

"I haven't." He paused, then just as she was starting to think he wasn't going to say more, he did. "I am unmated and have no children. Normally a centaur will only carry members of his family if they can't shift forms."

"This must be strange for you. I'm sorry."

He chuckled. "It does feel a bit odd. Carrying a rider is very different than a heavy load. You're warm for one thing, and I can feel you trying to match your motion to mine. That's nice. No pack, no matter how well loaded, will move like that."

"Guess I'm glad I'm more elegant than a sack of potatoes."

He chuckled again. "Yes. I'll just consider this practice for the eventuality I'll find a suitable mate one day."

"Glad to be of use," she directed at his spine.

Talking helped her to focus on something other than the centaur's body. While he was part horse, her mind was having trouble remembering that. With her arms wrapped around his waist and her breasts pressed against his back, it was hard to think about anything except how warm and human he felt.

She could feel every shift and flex of his muscle. Then he broke into a fast walk, and she was forced to concentrate on riding.

His gaits were slightly different than a horse's, she discovered. Smoother. Soon he was transitioning into a trot and then a canter.

"Are you ready to feel a centaur's speed, Warrior-

Priestess?" Toryn called over the rising sound of the wind.

"Aren't we moving fast now?"

He laughed. "No!"

A moment later, he broke into a gallop that was easily three times faster than anything she'd ever ridden.

"Oh, my Goddess!"

CHAPTER FOURTEEN

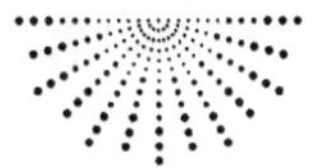

Toryn

With a journey of unknown length stretching out before him, Toryn admitted galloping at top speed to impress the pretty priestess on his back likely wasn't the smartest idea, but the way Seira had yelped in surprise and then clung to him was worth a little wasted energy.

But reason won out in the end, and he slowed from full gallop to a ground-eating cantor that he could keep up most of the day if he had to.

The slower pace had an unexpected result. Seira relaxed her guard around him and began to talk of inane things. Her horse. Her winter garden back in the fortress. Her friends and fellow priestesses. He noticed she didn't speak of her siblings; the topic was likely too painful.

"And what about you, Horseman? Why are you still a huntsman and not busy raising the next generation of little centaurs?"

He snorted and then found himself telling her the truth. "Because that's what my father wants. Thus, I'll keep doing the opposite."

Seira shifted, leaning out so she could see his face in profile. "Now you've whetted my appetite for gossip. It must be more than rebelling against a parent's wish to control. Half of all sires and dams are nosy and controlling. What makes yours worse?"

"He just is." Toryn sighed.

"Mm-hm."

But she was opening up even if it touched on a topic he didn't like talking about. After a moment, he released a gusty sigh.

"You're correct. It's more than just my father's influence. I have little interest in being part of a family herd. While I want little ones someday, and I don't doubt I'll enjoy the begetting of them with the right woman, I have no interest in sharing a female. If I'm going to give myself heart, mind, body, and soul to another, I want the same in return. I'm the jealous type. I don't share well."

He felt when more tension flowed from Seira's frame. He waited. At last, his patience was rewarded, and she began to converse once more.

"I've always wondered about how the centaurs handle the gender imbalance. So, you willingly share the women your kind capture?"

Toryn made a face. "Some more willing than others."

"And the women?" She wasn't able to hide the unease in her voice from him.

Feeling like a cad, Toryn reached down and instinctively patted her hands, where she was holding onto him. "We are not monsters. While the needs of our species' survival outweigh individual wants and desires, the life-bearers pick their mates from the herd of eligible males."

"They are allowed to choose?"

"Yes. From the available males. Not every male is a candidate. Each male must prove himself worthy."

"And how is that decided?"

Toryn chuckled. "Much as one would expect. Candidates prove their worth in contests of intellect and physical prowess. And then again later, they must show their potential mate those same abilities."

"The women your Hunts capture, they are not slaves, then?"

His lips compressed. He didn't want to cause a fissure to form in the new bridge of trust they'd started to build, but he didn't want to lie to her either.

Truth, even an unhappy one, was better than a lie, he decided. "While the women are treated very well—as many of their wants and needs met as possible—they are not free to leave us. Nor are the females allowed to take part in anything that might cause them harm. Their protection comes before our own. We need each woman if our race has any hope of surviving."

"Then they are pampered possessions with no real freedom?"

"Yes," he agreed. He wouldn't lie to sweeten the truth for Seira. "But we do what we must to survive what the soul-mages did to us."

"We are guilty of the same things as your people, Centaur," Seira said, surprising him. "Perhaps that makes both our peoples monsters. But neither race can ever come close to the monstrosities committed by the soul-mages."

He'd been sure she must think of centaurs as the enemy. Her pragmatism gave him hope.

"We both have responsibilities to our people. I've long understood that, and I've never held it against you.

You've always behaved in an honorable way." She paused and leaned to the side enough to gaze at him. "But that doesn't explain why you haven't captured me in all these years. You're skilled enough. You could have tracked me down and taken me unaware. I watched as you followed the path I'd taken through your camp that day at the river."

Toryn grinned. If she'd come upon him any later, it might have made for an even more awkward meeting. Many shifts to his human form ended in him thinking of Seira and what he wanted to do with her and to her.

"Well? Out with it, Horseman!"

He twitched at the command in her tone, but soon a grin was spreading across his lips again. Goddess of the Prairie, she was a fierce one. And she deserved to know the truth.

"I never want to see you in the possession of a male. To see that spark of wild fierceness die out of your eyes, to see you in a silken cage, no longer wild and free, that thought chills my soul. If I'd captured you, I would have destroyed a fundamental part of your spirit."

His words seemed to startle her into silence, and she didn't speak again for many of his strides. He remained silent. She'd talk when she was ready.

At last, she did.

"It's strange that a centaur, one I've always seen as a

rival, knows me better than the matrons of my people. I do not wish to give up my freedom or my battle magic. It's why I've turned down their offer to become one of the mothers."

"We're alike, Priestess." Toryn tilted his head so he could catch a glimpse of her out of the corner of his eye. "But you still haven't told me why *you* haven't tried to catch me to fulfill your duty to your people," Toryn challenged, turning the question on her. "You've found my camp many times. As much as it hurts my male pride to admit it, if you'd ever alerted one of your peoples' Hunts, I might have found myself a captive. It's curious that you never told one of the Hunt leaders where to find me, isn't it?"

Seira grunted. "Thank you for that reminder of how I have failed in my duty to my people by not capturing your arrogant ass years ago and delivering it to the matrons."

He snorted. "I think it's because you don't want to. You're not interested in turning me over to your people any more than I wish to see the same thing happen to you."

"You're not wrong," she said in a huff before suddenly biting out, "I would miss you."

Then she went on to tell him the rest, how she loved patrolling her land, hunting for her people, and protecting them from threats. She loved that duty too much to give it up. Like him, she enjoyed the freedom of having no one to answer to.

"Though, I'm beginning to fear the matrons might not take no for an answer much longer," Seira added.

"I fear the same from my father," Toryn admitted. "What are they holding over your head to force you to obey?"

She snorted with bitter humor. "Tradition. I'm born of one of the first Houses to swear allegiance to the Moon Goddess. As such, my bloodline is valued. But my two younger sisters were mature and ready to take mates before…." She swallowed audibly, drew in a shaky breath, and then continued in a stronger voice. "I thought I would have a few more years to walk my land, but now my sisters are gone. Only vengeance matters."

"And we will have our revenge," he promised. "But there is always more to life than pain and grief and revenge. One day you will heal."

"I don't know. I think if I'm cut off from the wilderness and forced to live in a city to see to my duty, a piece of my soul will always remain here in the wilds."

"I can understand that." He found he'd come to a stop. His eyes drifted closed, and he reached for where her hands were clasped around his waist. Her fingers were so much smaller than his. "We are both attuned to this land. It's in our souls. It makes up a core part of our essence. That's why I'm still here even against my father's wishes."

Seira sighed and squeezed his fingers. "I would miss our games if I ever allowed another to capture you," she said, her voice thick with emotions. She cleared her throat. "It would be the same if I left to become a mother."

"I enjoy our little games as well," he admitted, wanting to tell her more, to say that she was the only woman he wanted.

"Good. It's settled then." She cleared her throat a second time. "For the duration of this mission, we are partners. After it's over, we'll return the souls of our people to the elders so they can free them. Then we will return to our posts."

"That's it?" He couldn't hide some of the disappointment he felt.

She shrugged. "We'll continue to guard our lands as we always have."

He grunted, one eyebrow arched, and he could feel where his lips curled in a quizzical look. "And?"

Seira would soon learn the depth of his stubbornness. But he didn't think he'd have to hold out long this time to get what he wanted. She wanted it as well, even if she didn't fully understand what was between them.

He'd simply have to wait her out.

"Fine, Horseman. No doubt we'll occasionally cross the river to get up to mischief."

When he twisted to give her a great big grin, he noted the flush crawling up her cheeks. He reminded himself to give her his most infectious smile as often as possible.

Now that he'd gotten that much of an agreement out of her, it was time to go in for the kill.

"And what if we decide we like each other's company on this journey?"

Even a maiden priestess had to know precisely what he was asking. His kind weren't subtle in nature or body language.

Smiling serenely, she answered him, "You're welcome to cross the river and have tea at my fire, Centaur. Just tea. Nothing more. Don't want you getting your hopes up—or anything else—over the invitation."

Toryn chuckled. "Very well. I'll accept tea."

He was confident she understood his unspoken 'for now' following the last word.

CHAPTER FIFTEEN

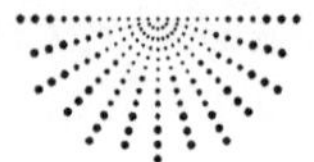

Seira

The next two days were a blur. But Toryn hadn't lied. A centaur really could travel much faster than a horse and needed less rest. The tracks were still visible. Though Seira was beginning to worry. The signs were fading.

But Toryn's swift pace was narrowing the distance between them and their prey. In another day, two at the most, Seira would be close enough to use her magic to track the souls of her people. Then they would run down the enemy.

And even when they were both tired, Toryn was a good-natured travel companion. Usually, if she had to travel with another for any length of time, she wanted time alone, but she didn't feel the same need to seek out solitude while in the centaur's company. He was naturally serene.

And yet when she craved conversation to take her mind off the grief that would creep in when she was alone with her own thoughts, Toryn would somehow sense her mood and offer a verbal distraction.

She was just concluding she was already growing attached to the centaur when he skidded to a halt so swiftly, she nearly cracked her forehead against his muscular back.

He raised a hand for silence. She obeyed, already straining her senses, trying to discover what she'd missed. After a few moments of hearing nothing except her and the centaur's breathing, she detected the faint sound of hoofbeats.

"Horses, not centaurs," she whispered in his ear so softly the sound didn't carry. From spying on him all these years, she'd gotten skilled enough to detect the subtle difference between a horse's and a centaur's hoofbeats. "At least ten. It has to be a Hunting party from Highrock."

He nodded. "Will you know them?"

"Possibly. But it could also be women I've never met. It would be better to avoid them."

He nodded. "Unfortunately, there isn't time to hide my path and backtrack far enough that they won't discover the trail."

Seira grunted in displeasure. He was correct, though. If they'd been in their territories, they'd know all the trails with hard-packed ground too firm to take a print or how to escape any pursuit using the network of streams and rivers to disappear.

"They're going to find us," she concluded. "Let me do the talking."

"Gladly," Toryn agreed. "But let me try to slip through their line. Perhaps our goddesses will be merciful and allow us to outrun them?"

CHAPTER SIXTEEN

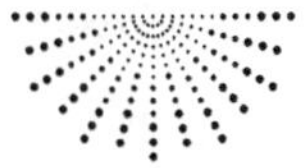

Toryn

Apparently neither of their goddesses were in a merciful mood, and Toryn was beginning to wonder what he'd done to anger his deity. He skidded to a halt for the third time as he spun on his heels and darted in a new direction.

More net-carrying women on horseback were charging at him from the south and west as well. But that wasn't the nearest danger. Cursing, he leaped to the side as his instincts warned him a moment before a net fell from the tree directly overhead.

He kept one hand on Seira's knee to help hold her in

place as he spun again and darted off in a different direction.

"You can't outrun them," Seira shouted. "They have us surrounded. Stop and let me talk to them!"

She was likely correct, but he never gave in.

"I'll explain our mission, warn them about the soul-mages. They aren't foolish. They'll understand the danger of allowing the soul-mages to escape with whatever they've learned of our defenses. They'll aid us in our hunt."

He trusted Seira, and he knew she wasn't lying to him. Not intentionally. But he didn't think the other women would just let him escape after the mission was complete either.

But just then, three more fierce warriors on horseback were charging at him with nets at the ready.

Cursing, he spun and galloped in a new direction. Then he cursed again. At his fate this time. It was certain. He'd done something to annoy a god. He'd worry about that later.

For now, he had a sticky situation to escape.

As it turned out, it looked like he'd walked into the exact patch of forest where three separate Hunts had been gathering to share plans to capture any centaur huntsman in the area.

Unfortunately, he was the only centaur huntsman

foolish enough to cross their territory during the Hunting Moon. But this was the direction the soul-mages had traveled. He didn't have a choice but to follow.

"Toryn, if you break a leg in this mad dash through the forest, how will that help free the souls of your people?"

She had a point.

But to stop running was to admit defeat and surrender his freedom. And if that happened, the women of the mountain would use their magic to steal his equine form, locking it away. He'd be trapped in the form of a man for the rest of his days.

That terrified him.

"Toryn, do you trust me?" Seira asked in a whisper, her lips close to his ear.

"Yes, but..."

"Then trust me to find a way to help you escape once our mission is over." She reached down and squeezed his one hand where it was gripping her knee to help her stay on. "I won't betray you or fail to carryout my promise. I give you my word."

"You swear?" While Toryn delighted in any number of night fantasies about a certain warrior-priestess attempting to master him, he had no interest in playing stud to a harem. Certainly not when the price was to lose his centaur nature as well as his freedom. But did he really have a choice?

She leaned forward until her lips were brushing his mobile ears. "I swear I'll find a way to set you free."

Huffing in displeasure—and maybe a little fear, he admitted to himself—he slowed and then halted.

It didn't take the women hunting them long to approach and encircle him.

"I wish to speak with the Hunt leader immediately," Seira barked out the order, and Toryn noticed they jumped to attention.

"Maiden…" The closest of the women prompted.

"Maiden Seira of House Blackstone," she supplied.

Toryn noted the woman in the lead straightened at Seira's title. And well they should. House Blackstone was the oldest of the clan houses, and while the women of the mountains didn't have a single ruling monarch— they had a triumvirate of queens—Seira was of royal blood.

"You will hear me out," Seira continued in her tone of authority. "This centaur is not to be mistreated. He is an ally. The soul-mages have returned. They've already massacred one of our Hunts and one belonging to the centaurs as well."

Seira's news was met with gasps of surprise and

more questions and demands. Soon members from three different Hunts were arranged around Toryn.

Even with the news of the soul-mages to distract them, he didn't like how some of them were sizing him up.

Toryn hoped Seira was damn good at negotiations.

CHAPTER SEVENTEEN

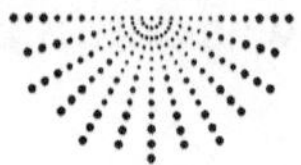

Seira

After Seira had said her piece and the fiery-haired matron still ordered Toryn to be hobbled, Seira decided it was good she wasn't a matron of her House. She was terrible at negotiations.

It likely didn't help that a matron rode with one of the Hunts. It was unusual, but their scouts had reported seeing tracks from a strange company of riders.

Matron Brisdarra had been dispatched from Highrock to investigate. When she'd confirmed the tacks were neither centaur nor of her own people, she'd summoned two other Hunts.

Which was the trap she and Toryn had stumbled into. Though they weren't the intended targets.

"Soul-mages," Matron Brisdarra whispered, her skin turning pale, making her freckles standout in contrast. "Since the horses were shod, unlike our mountain ponies, I assumed these were raiders or pirates from the old world. It never occurred to me that I might be looking at tracks made by soul-mages. Goddess. I thought they'd all died out. No one has seen or heard of a soul-mage in over two hundred years."

"We were not so fortunate for them to have died out," Seira confirmed.

Seira had already explained how she and Toryn had come upon the two massacred Hunts. Blessedly, Matron Brisdarra believed them and agreed that the soul-mages must be hunted down.

"It's imperative that you release Toryn. Only a centaur has a chance of catching up to the soul-mages. They have too much of a head start as it is. Every moment we waste debating allows them to slip farther away."

"That may be true; however, I can't let you risk a captured centaur who is capable of fathering many babies upon the women of the mountains to merely rescue a few souls. There's a good chance you both would die. The soul-mages would then collect your souls and still escape." Matron Brisdarra nodded to the other members of the Hunt around them. "I will split our force. Half will go with you to hunt down the soul-mages. The rest will travel with the centaur back to our fortress to make sure he is safeguarded."

"And how will our slower horses catch up to the invaders?" Seira was holding back her growing rage. She was concerned for Toryn, but she didn't dare show that to the others. They had to believe all her concern was for retrieving her sisters' souls. Which did fill her heart with worry, but that didn't mean she couldn't also be concerned for her new centaur partner.

Brisdarra just brushed off Seira's concern. "Winter is coming early to the mountains this year. If the soul-mages return the way they came—and as far as we can tell, they have—then they will find a surprise when they reach the mountains." The matron's tone was extremely confident. "Once there, they'll find their horses are no match for our sturdy mountain ponies in the snow and bad footing."

That might be true. But Seira couldn't risk her sisters' souls on something as fickle as the weather. It was common for winter to spread an early dusting or even a heavy fall of snow and then disappear for a moon's cycle.

But if the good weather returned, then it would be

the soul-mages disappearing as their boat sailed off across the ocean.

Fury building within her, Seira wanted to reach out and wrap her fingers around the other woman's throat and throttle her. She took several calming breaths instead. An emotional outburst wouldn't win Toryn his freedom.

"The centaur is too valuable. He remains our guest. And I will send half the Hunt with you to help you destroy the soul-mage invaders and rescue the trapped souls. That is my final word on this matter."

Seira wouldn't allow that, but it was time for a change in strategy.

Instead of the angry retort she wanted to respond with, she merely nodded her head.

Then Seira allowed her gaze to intentionally linger on Toryn, her look more of a caress. Then she turned to glower at the Matron of Highrock.

"He is mine. I had planned to capture him after we completed our mission. And while I will share him for the good of all, he is the property of House Blackstone, but any of the women who took part in his hunt are welcome to journey to my home and prove themselves worthy of such a fine specimen. But I will have the first taste and choose who else receives the honor of courting him."

CHAPTER EIGHTEEN

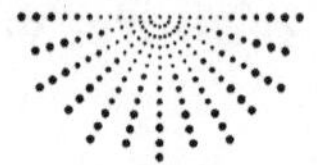

Seira

Seira wasn't surprised when the other woman smirked at her declaration about Toryn's purpose and fate. He was a fine-looking male. One of the finest she'd seen.

"I can't make promises once he's in our home fortress," Matron Brisdarra drawled.

Seira drew her knife and swiftly pressed the blade against the other woman's throat before she could react. "I am the most skilled of the warrior-priestesses. The only reason I am not a mother or a matron of greater rank than you is because I've chosen not to take up that particular mantle of leadership yet. Instead, I have chosen to protect my people by guarding our borders. Do not mistake that as a lack of determination or ambition. Tell the others of my claim, and if any of them think to have first taste, tell them no man's cock will ever stir for them again once I'm finished carving up their faces in punishment."

She stroked her dagger back and forth along the other woman's cheek. "Do I make myself clear?"

The matron swallowed nervously. "It will be as you say. You have my word. I will see that he is protected with my life."

"Good." Seira lowered the knife. "Once I return, I will select other worthy priestesses to receive his potent seed. Do you have a daughter among this Hunt?"

"I do," Matron Brisdarra said slowly.

"Good. If you please me in your protection of the male, I will make sure one of your daughters is among the chosen for his harem."

The matron stood a little straighter. "Darbrina, come forward. A scion of House Blackstone wishes to speak with you."

A pale-skinned woman with blonde hair and blue eyes came forward. Seira could see the centaur bloodlines ran strong in this female; she had none of her mother's freckles or red hair. That particular shade of silver-blue eyes was much more common among centaurs and humans born of centaur fathers.

Not that anyone was pureblood human stalk after several generations of crossbreeding with the centaurs, but centaur blood was stronger in some Houses than others. Seira's own house was rich with centaur blood, but like her, most of the women had darker skin and black hair and eyes.

As Seira studied the other woman as if to gauge her worthiness to breed with a centaur of such prime stalk as Toryn, she watched the woman for different reasons, looking for weaknesses.

The woman licked her lips, nervousness warring with greed. Seira was offering to align a lesser house with House Blackstone. And that was no little thing.

Many a woman would jump at the chance to join one of the founding Houses, and competition for males was steep. To be offered a position of such high rank was a tantalizing treat. But it could be deadly as well. More than one woman had died in the noble halls of Fortress Blackstone from a competitor's blade.

Such violence was frowned upon, of course. But that didn't stop it from happening. Greed and lust were powerful motivators.

Brisdarra's daughter was likely debating her chances.

But in the end, greed won out as she ran her gaze along Toryn's muscular chest. She nodded.

Matron Brisdarra turned from her daughter to look upon Seira. "We accept your offer. May the Moon Goddess bless your generosity. House Highrock will forever be in your debt."

Seira muttered a few niceties at the matron, but her gaze was on the daughter. She didn't like the way the other woman was gazing at Toryn like he was a sweet treat she just couldn't wait to start licking. The cause wasn't hard to guess.

As part of a Hunt, all the members were required to go off their daily fertility suppressing tea. One of the side effects of going off the magic laced herbal mix was a surge of hormones and the return of natural hungers and heated needs.

Seira sneered. Hormones seemed like very inconvenient distractions. She was glad she always carried a large store of the herb in her pack. There was enough to get her to the ocean and then back to her home territory with some to spare.

The last thing she needed was to lose her head over a male.

"Very well, Darbrina," Seira drawled. "All is settled then. I will leave you and a company of your choice to watch over and protect our soon to be mate while your mother and I scout the area to be certain there are no other soul-mages in the vicinity."

Matron Brisdarra made a harrumphing sound. "We have already found the tracks of the invaders and determined they are at least three days old."

"And are you certain there was only one group of soul-mages?" Seira snapped at the other woman. "I'm not. And I'm certainly not going to risk another group coming upon us unaware. I've burned enough bodies. I don't plan on becoming the next victim. You will pick out the best hunters and trackers, and we will patrol a large area around the rest of the camp tonight. There will be no more surprises."

"Very well, Maiden Blackstone. Your will shall be carried out."

Seira nodded, and then her gaze darted to Toryn.

His eyes met hers over the distance, two burning embers of icy grey-blue rage boring into her.

It was clear he thought she'd betrayed him. But she was doing what she had to do to protect him. Unfortunately, there was no way to convey her plans to him with the others looking on.

And she most certainly had plans for herself and the centaur that didn't involve taking him anywhere near one of her peoples' fortresses.

CHAPTER NINETEEN

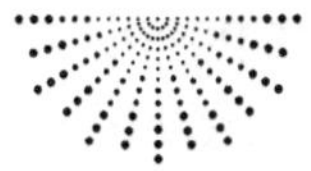

Seira

After pulling arrogance around her shoulders like a mantle, Seira had stood near enough to Toryn to oversee his treatment while Matron Brisdarra and several of her women went about securing the centaur to the tree.

Then after he was hobbled and tried by many stout ropes, Seira and the matron had set out on patrol leading a good two-thirds of the other women.

Once they were all in place, the camp would be as safe as anywhere outside of one of the fortress cities.

Which was the only reason Seira was willingly leaving Toryn while he was tied up and helpless.

And if there had been any possibility of a soul-mage near, she never would have left his side. As it was, she didn't like it, but she had a part to play—the dutiful Huntress protecting her people and the valuable centaur she'd managed to trick into aiding her.

It all left a bad taste in her mouth.

Though there was another reason she didn't like leaving Toryn behind. Before she'd left, she'd noticed the women remaining behind were eyeing the centaur with a great deal of interest.

No doubt having a handsome centaur helpless in their keeping would likely be a little too much for some of the women to resist.

While Toryn might be accosted by a few amorous women, he was in centaur form, so there wasn't much fun they could get up to. Toryn would survive a few unskilled kisses and caresses, she reminded herself.

That knowledge did little to help her unclench her jaw, though.

But eventually those women would sleep. When they did, it would make escaping with Toryn that much easier. By the time the women on guard duty returned, she and the centaur would be far away.

She sent a mental prayer to her goddess.

Her plan had to work because she wouldn't leave her partner to his fate. She'd given him her word that she wouldn't capture him and turn him over to the matrons.

She was just beginning to mull over a second plan of escape if the first failed when her gaze landed on a familiar plant. She'd only noticed it because a stray moonbeam had penetrated the forest canopy overhead like a message from her goddess. Her breath caught.

Bronze-royal was named after its similar coloring to its coin namesake. It was a rare and valuable plant. Its many medicinal properties included speed with healing, pain reduction, and it could even put a patient to sleep when its seeds were steeped.

She just as swiftly looked away from the plant, not wanting to draw Brisdarra's attention to it.

"I'll hunt us a deer for dinner tonight, and then I'll take first watch," Seira told the other woman. "I'd feel better if you went back and secured my prize. I don't want him escaping now that he knows what I have planned for him, thanks to your interference."

The other woman snorted. "He would have figured it out swiftly enough on his own once you trapped him in the form of a man and had your way with him."

Seira only barely managed to keep a snarl off her lips. She knew of the spells the matron spoke of, but she hadn't yet had reason to learn them. And honestly, no desire to do so even if that knowledge had been offered to her. But she had to say something to the other woman.

"Still, he knows the truth now and will be looking to escape long before we get him back to a fortress."

"There is that. And he was a hard one to catch even when you were on his back." The other woman sighed. "I can only imagine how much more trouble he'll be free of any load. I'll return to watch over our prize."

"Thank you, Matron."

The other woman nodded and then turned her gelding and headed back the way they'd come.

Seira waited until she could no longer hear the horse's hooves in the distance before dismounting to gather the bronze-royal. When her borrowed mount's saddlebags were bulging, she set out to find dinner.

Later, she'd baste the deer with the herb and see if she could sneak some of its seeds in to mull with the wine as it heated over the fire.

Then once everyone was drugged, Seira would free the centaur and lead him to safety. From there, they would continue their journey.

CHAPTER TWENTY

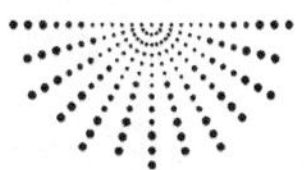

Toryn

$\mathcal{A}$ banked fury burning in his chest, Toryn watched as another female turned from where she sat around one of the cooking fires to gaze at him. Her eyes were already bright with determination, and as he watched, she downed the last of her wine.

He flashed her his teeth. The look was anything but friendly. It seemed to work, for the female sat back down at the fire and poured herself another drink.

He cast a look around, searching for Seira.

"Why am I even looking?" He muttered to himself. "I shouldn't care where she is or what she's doing."

He'd been a fool for trusting her as much as he had.

A small, foolish part of his heart still hoped this was all an elaborate act on her part. But even if it was, he didn't know how she'd manage to help him escape.

He was being watched all the time by no less than ten sets of eyes.

And at present, two more women were walking in his direction with a determination that suggested they were planning on doing more than look.

The taller of the two, a lovely dark-skinned female, knelt in front of him.

"Hello there, pretty man. I don't suppose we can convince you to shapeshift into a more useful form?"

"No."

She leaned back and gave him another smirk. "No matter. My older sister is already a mother, and she taught me the spells of change that can force a centaur to shift. Does that sound fun?"

"Not really." He managed to fill the words with disdain. Too bad he wasn't feeling as confident in reality. A shiver of doubt had invaded his confidence the moment she told him about the spell.

He knew from the accounts of the few males who had escaped from the women of the mountains that once trapped in human form, his chances of escape would diminish greatly.

Now he was regretting not fighting harder to escape when he was first captured. But protective instincts had stopped him from harming any of the women in his bid for freedom. And he'd trusted Seira, listening to her reasoning until he'd surrendered. But he now feared her promise to help procure his freedom was a lie.

Goddess of the Prairies! What a fool he'd been.

But the two mountain women were unaware of his thoughts and merely smiled at him as they began discarding articles of clothing.

Gritting his teeth, Toryn did his best to ignore the rich brown skin and dark nipples of the one he'd labeled as the leader, but turning his head just put him in line to see her paler skinned companion's high, firm breasts.

Toryn snarled as they settled next to him.

His growl did startle them enough they jerked back. But the reprieve didn't last long. Soon they were whispering among themselves.

When the paler skinned one leaned forward and placed her palms against his chest and began to chant in a singsong tone, he knew he was in trouble.

While his centaur body could only be aroused by a mate's touch, his human form was much easier to convince, and by the tingle running along his body, their spell was already interacting with his natural shapeshifting magic.

He was in trouble.

And tied as he was, once he shifted to human form, he'd still be limited in how quickly he could subdue these two women. There was another problem. As soon as he overpowered both of them, more women would come to their rescue.

He wasn't at all sure the new rescuers wouldn't continue where these two had left off.

"You're a handsome one. I can't wait to feel your power, to finally know what it's like."

"I can." His nostrils flared, but not in pleasure. "Where is Seira? She had right of first reward for my capture. Not you."

She pulled back to study him, her gaze intense. But this female was nothing like his Seira. Even as angry as he was with Seira right now, he'd much rather it was her here planning to seduce him. That he would enjoy at least.

This?

This wasn't going to be enjoyable at all. He closed his eyes to shut off that one sense.

Just when he thought he'd have to endure having indignities done to him, one of the women screamed suddenly.

Toryn snapped his gaze up in time to see Seira grab

the woman by her throat. Then Seira made one long slash on the other woman's face from ear to chin.

"That is so you will remember your stupidity this night when you wake each morning," Seira snarled the words at them, sounding more menacing than he'd ever heard her.

And just like that, his body warmed at Seira's fierceness.

Goddess. She was so fierce and protective of him. He liked it. He really shouldn't, but he did.

Nothing should please him about the situation he found himself in.

But Seira wasn't like these other females.

She was his perfect mate.

And right now, she was stalking over to him, dismissing her rivals.

When she reached his side, she leaned down and blew softly on his ear. It was so unexpected, he jerked at the contact. But she only met his eyes in an intense look, trying to convey something to him. He wasn't sure what.

She slipped her arms around his waist and then pressed closer to kiss him. Her lips were warm and soft, so soft. And unskilled, but he loved that too. His anger started to fade, replaced by something else he'd be wise to resist.

But just then, she broke away from his lips and licked a path to his ear, and he didn't want to resist.

A barely heard whisper caressed his ear along with her hot breath. "I'm going to cut partway through your ropes. Not all the way through. Don't want someone to notice. But I also want you to be able to free yourself if someone else tries to accost you again if I'm not here to stop it."

He felt her fingers skate down his arms until she was stroking the inside of his wrists. The sensations that simple touch stirred in him were surprising in their intensity.

He returned her kisses. It was supposed to be play-acting, but he'd waited so long for this, it was anything but playful on his part. His arms flexing with the need to enfold her, he jerked on his ropes.

"Not yet. You'll give away my plan." She made a pretense of nipping his ear playfully. Tugging on it, she pulled back very slightly. "I've drugged the wine and meat. Don't eat or drink any if they offer it to you. I said I'd take first watch. But what I'll really be watching for is when they're asleep. Once they are, I'll return. We'll make our escape then."

She touched his lips, and this time, he returned her caresses ever more eagerly. Yes, he reminded himself, she might only be acting. But that didn't mean he wasn't enjoying her soft touches even more now that he knew she'd not betrayed him like he'd thought.

"Forgive me for doubting you, my lovely Huntress."

Seira snorted and then bit at his jaw as she slid the hilt of a small knife between his bound hands.

"That's enough for now," she said loudly enough to carry as she pulled back. "I volunteered for first watch. You make me regret that now."

With one last caress of her fingers along his human abdomen, she turned and marched swiftly away. He enjoyed the view as the tip of her braid thumped against the curve of her backside. He vowed one day that she would be his.

With nothing else to do, he prepared himself for a wait.

CHAPTER TWENTY-ONE

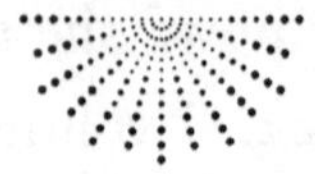

Seira

Picking her way between the sprawled bodies of the hunting party, Seira headed toward Toryn's location. He was even now cutting through the ropes binding his equine lower body.

"You all right?" she asked as he rose to his feet.

He nodded sharply and took the weapons and packs she handed him. While he was buckling on his weapon harness and armor, she strapped his other harness in place and secured their packs and supplies. She already wore all her weapons.

Once everything was in place, he twisted to the side

and cupped his hands. She took the offer of help and vaulted onto his back, and then they were off.

He paused at the edge of the light as if something occurred to him.

"The fires and torches should burn for a while yet," she commented, reading the concern in his expression. "The women should be safe enough from most four-legged predators."

"And are you not worried about others of my kind finding them?"

Seira grunted. "It will serve them right if a centaur hunting party happens upon them."

Toryn twisted to glance over his shoulder at her. "Remind me not to get on your bad side."

She flashed teeth at him. "Well, if they'd just kept their noses out of my business, or better yet, actually had offered to aid us and not abducted my partner, it would have turned out much better for all. But they interfered with me rescuing the souls of my younger sisters. They paid the price for being greedy."

"I thank you for honoring your word to me," Toryn said and flashed her one of his boyish smiles she found so devastating.

With a low growling huff to hide her embarrassment, she nodded. "It's not your fault we mountain women get hormonal when we first go off the tea. It's like years of pent up desire awakens, I'm told. That's another reason I've turned down becoming a Mother. I don't ever want to lose control of myself, even just that much. Sex hormones make people stupid."

Toryn started to laugh at her words. "I won't deny that. Many a centaur has allowed himself to be led around by the tug of his nether region."

It was Seira's turn to laugh. Once she had herself under control, she gave his shoulders a firm smack. "I never thought I'd say this, but we think alike, Centaur."

"I'll take that as the greatest of compliments."

Yes, it was. Seira didn't care for most people, but the centaur was a fine travel companion.

Wrapping her arms more firmly around his waist, she grinned at his back.

CHAPTER TWENTY-TWO

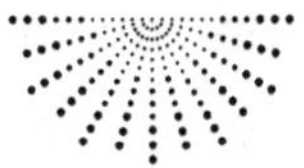

Seira

They continued to follow the trail left by the soul-mages even as the signs grew fainter. That worried Seira. It could only mean the soul-mages had found fresh mounts and were increasing the distance. Either they knew where to steal new mounts, or they'd already planned ahead and had left fresh mounts with a few of their number somewhere in the foothills.

Neither option was good. It meant she and Toryn were now even farther behind than they'd hoped. Toryn didn't seem overly troubled by the news. Though he increased his pace as he scanned the ground ahead for signs of the invaders' trail.

Even with Toryn's dogged determination, Seira couldn't help the niggle of doubt that kept creeping into her mind during idle moments.

And she couldn't help but dwell on how the one day they'd been stuck with the hunting party was a day too long, and because of that, Seira might lose her chance to rescue the souls of her sisters. That knowledge made a clammy, cold sweat bead up along her sides.

Toryn slowed suddenly.

She peered around his shoulder to see they'd come to a fork.

"Matron Brisdarra guessed correctly," he said. "They went right, taking the mountain pass instead of the longer, but easier, routine through the lowlands."

Seira nodded. Both pleased that Toryn was still able to follow the trail so well, but also uneasy to know the enemy had taken the harder route. It left her and her centaur partner that much less time to run them down and set in motion their plan to cut out around the group and lay traps and other nasty surprises for the soul-mages.

But a moment later, she reassured herself. The

highest snow-capped peaks were still far away. Even from their position in the foothills, she could see snow already descending down toward the valleys. Winter was coming, and the snows would slow the enemy.

"We follow them," Seira said into the silence. "We have no choice."

"I know," Toryn agreed. But he didn't continue down the path. "We must stop here to rest before we take on the mountains."

For the first time in days, worry for his ability to maintain his swift pace swept over her. He'd held up so well, seemingly able to run near tirelessly all day, every day, that she'd grown accustomed to his power and stamina and had stopped questioning it.

But no creature could maintain such a pace without injury indefinitely.

"What's wrong?" Seira swung down from his back and began running her hands along his legs. "Are you hurt? Going lame?"

She continued to run her hands along his legs, seeking hot spots or swelling. After a thorough search revealed nothing, she looked back up at him with suspicion.

His tail flagged behind him, and he nearly pranced in place. His smirking grin reminded her he wasn't a horse and she shouldn't treat him like one. And she'd just been running her hands all over him. She pulled her hands away like she'd burned them.

"You're not lame at all, are you?" she growled.

"Lame? No."

"You could have told me that sooner."

"And missed out on my chance to have your hands on me?"

She growled and smacked him on the rump.

Leaping away, he grinned harder. Once he had his laughter under control, he told her what she wanted to know.

"I'm not lame. But I might as well be. The rest will be almost as long as if I bruised a hoof," he grumbled. "A centaur can only maintain his true form for so many consecutive days before he loses the ability to shift to human form."

"Oh." She hadn't known that. Though it explained why some of the captured centaurs strongest in magic would still eventually revert to human forms even when the spells of the matrons failed to force the shift. "How long do you need?"

"I can sleep in my human form tonight and return to my true form in the morning. If forced, I could put off shifting for another day or two without endangering myself, but I'd rather shift now before we're in the mountains with hungry cats. Mountain lions have no love for centaur hooves."

He grinned and stomped one front hoof against the ground as if crushing an invisible skull.

CHAPTER TWENTY-THREE

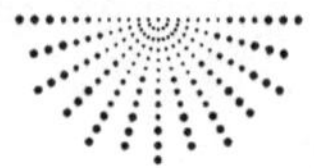

Seira

Toryn waited until after they'd set up camp on a windswept patch of relatively flat ground. The tent rattled in the wind, but Seira had made doubly sure the grounding stakes were pounded well. The last thing they'd need was for Toryn's centaur-sized tent to uproot itself and roll down the slope or blow farther down the valley.

Once the tent was set up and they'd gathered enough wood to fuel a small cooking fire, Toryn retreated into the tent to shift forms. She didn't blame him. She would have gone into the tent to shift as well if she'd been him.

The evening was bone-chillingly cold, and the constant wind only made matters worse.

While she'd seen him in human form, she'd never witnessed his actual shift. She was curious but not so forthright, not to mention rude, to just boldly march into the tent to watch.

Though knowing the centaur, he would have welcomed a chance to allow her to gaze upon all he had to offer. Even without making her feel threatened, he still managed to be blatantly obvious about his willingness to take their unique partnership to the next level.

Well, he could just toss that thought in the fire. She was more than content with things the way they were.

After fidgeting outside the closed tent flap, she walked back to the fire and tossed on a couple more logs. Then she picked up her bow and quiver and paused outside the tent again.

"Toryn," she had to shout over the roar of the wind, "I'm going to go find some fresh meat for dinner. I've already set the kettle on a rock next to the fire if you want something hot to drink before I get back."

"I could come with you." His voice was muffled by the tent fabric and the wind, but she could still hear him.

"No need. You can man the fire. I won't be gone long. I saw lots of rabbits on our way up here."

"Fine. Watch out for big cats."

"I will, Mother." She grinned when a humorous snort reached her ears.

～

Her hunt was a success, and soon she was back at camp with three fat rabbits. Toryn was sitting by the fire wrapped in a blanket and drinking tea.

As she approached, she noticed his frame shaking with cold.

"Why don't you go inside the tent while I cook these," she offered. "The wind won't be able to get you in there, at least."

"Feels colder inside," he hunched lower as a second shiver raced down his body.

Narrowing her eyes, she studied him for a long moment. "What's wrong? Tell the truth."

His teeth began chattering as he forced words between his lips.

"I've burned through a lot of my natural reserves. And since I hadn't expected to be traveling this deep into the mountains, I didn't bring as warm of blankets as I should have. Didn't want the extra weight to slow us down." He shivered again. "I'll be fine."

Seira narrowed her eyes. The stubborn horse's ass wasn't going to be okay, but warm food would be good for him, so she swiftly began preparing the rabbits and soon had them cooking over the fire. Next, she pulled out a small pot and diced some peppers, potatoes, and carrots she'd brought with her for stew. She'd learned centaurs loved carrots almost as much as a true horse did.

Once dinner was on, she turned and walked to their shared tent to retrieve the other blanket. Then she moved to Toryn's side of the fire and settled her blanket around his shoulders as well.

"No," he said as he tried to push the blanket toward her. "You'll need that."

She merely draped it back around his shoulders a second time and then grabbed a corner and settled next to him so they could share body heat under the two blankets.

After wrapping one arm around his waist, she tugged him closer. "Come here before you freeze to death. Your body is going into shock. I might not be far into my healer's training, but I know an overtaxed body when I see one."

The centaur didn't need more encouragement. His arm slid around her shoulders, and he buried his face in her neck.

"So damn cold," he mumbled.

"I know. You'll be warm soon." Moving her hand

from around his waist, she began to rub his back in a quick up and down movement. Then after a moment, she used her other hand to briskly rub his nearest thigh from hip to knee. They were the easiest parts of him she could reach to help get his blood flowing.

Toryn moaned and nearly melted into her touch.

She laughed but continued her ministrations. "Get ahold of yourself, Centaur. I'm just touching your back and leg. Nothing to get excited about."

"Your touch is always something to get excited about," he countered.

Rolling her eyes, she continued to rub warmth back into his body. Once his shivering had subsided, she left him with the two blankets so she could tend to their evening meal. Once dinner had been tended to, she hurried back to sit with him under the blanket.

He eagerly wrapped her in his arms and dragged her into his lap. She sensed his mood had changed; his not so subtle touch soon became more heated caresses.

"Horseman," she warned, putting a little more bite in her tone.

"But my plan would warm us up nicely," he countered.

Sighing, she slipped her hand down his chest in a caress. While Toryn's eager sound of encouragement did something to her she shouldn't even acknowledge, it didn't distract her from her task.

Before he knew what she was about, one of her long, thin blades was in her hand, the tip between their bodies, pressing against his groin.

"You are an absolutely lovely male to look upon. I'd hate to spoil all the beautiful potential by gelding you. Why don't you just sit and relax and absorb all the heat I'm so generously sharing with you without making trouble."

"You made your point. I shall behave." Toryn's rich laughter floated away on the breeze.

At least he was happier and warmer, she mused.

Horny she could deal with.

His death she couldn't.

If he continued to react near her, then he'd just have to respond and deal with the ache, because she wasn't going to let him freeze to death or break her own sacred vows just to scratch an itch.

CHAPTER TWENTY-FOUR

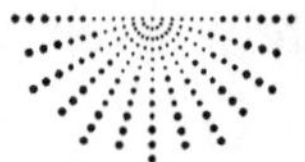

Toryn

Over the last three days, he'd carried the priestess higher into the mountains in the pursuit of the soul-mages. The foothills had soon given way to taller peaks where winter had come early. Even with his upper body wrapped in a fur-lined vest and a long shirt, the cold still found ways to crawl into seams and openings to run cold fingers along his skin.

Why couldn't nature have given him a sensible full-body coat instead of just covering his equine lower body? Though, being hairless had been a benefit in the warmer climates. The feel of Seira's arms around his waist and the soft press of her against his back more than made up for a little discomfort in colder temperatures.

"Why couldn't they have taken the pass that headed to the lowlands?" Seira grumbled.

"Are you cold? We can stop for a short time if you wish."

They weren't dressed for this kind of weather, and they'd had to stop early each night and a couple times throughout the day to warm up before a fire or risk frostbite.

At night, sharing blankets snug inside his tent was a delight even if he was in centaur form. Each night after she'd fallen asleep, he took her in his arms. He loved the feel of her, the rise and fall of her chest, the soft exhale of warm breath against his neck, her wandering hands.

Goddess. He loved her wandering hands.

Even though she slept fully clothed, he could still feel her plump breasts and womanly curves.

And each night in his dreams, he stripped off all her layers until her lovely full breasts were exposed to his sight, and he could run his hands along her sides and down her back. The imagined lovemaking sessions always began with him worshiping her body, showing her that there was more to life than chaste servitude to a cold goddess.

"Toryn!"

He jerked like she'd hit him.

What? What had he missed?

He scanned his surroundings with more care and soon spotted what had alerted her to danger moments later.

"It's a body," Seira whispered in his ear a moment before she was swinging down from his back.

Her bow was out a moment later. He drew his ax from his harness and together they approached the body.

Toryn knew it was already dead and frozen but still used a foreleg to prod the body. No traps, magical or physical, surrounded the corpse.

"It's safe," he said a moment later after flipping over the body.

Seira knelt, careful not to get her knees in the snow.

Toryn kept a watchful eye as she searched the body.

"His left arm is broken," she said. "He's banged up quite badly, but none of those injuries would have killed him quickly if he'd found shelter. It looks like he died of exposure after being caught in the storm." Seira paused and glanced around. "It's lucky we found him at all. The wind likely kept the snow off him."

Trotting a slow circle around her and the body, Toryn hunted for other corpses. He came to a rise in the land and then halted. "I think I know what killed him."

Seira joined him and gazed down into the valley floor choked with snow, broken trees, and even boulders. An avalanche had swept down from higher up the slopes not that long ago.

"Avalanches are very rare this early in the season," Seira mentioned as she scanned the valley floor.

He snorted, another idea coming to him. "Perhaps one of our gods or goddesses took affront at the atrocities commented by the soul-mages."

"Perhaps," she agreed before turning back to the body.

Toryn resumed his search for more carcasses. Though he wondered how many of them were even now trapped at the bottom of the valley under a mountainside's worth of snow.

He certainly wouldn't grieve their deaths, but it would make retrieving the stolen souls much more difficult. But Seira wasn't discouraged, and neither was he. If the soul-mages had perished down there, then they would never escape with the souls of his and the priestess's people.

It might take until the spring melt to find all the bodies and the soul crystals they carried, but Toryn wouldn't stop searching until he found them all.

Seira deserved to have the peace of knowing her loved ones were at last free to make the journey to the afterlife.

A few moments of searching and Seira was calling his name.

He turned back to her and spotted the glowing icy-blue crystal suspended from a heavy silver chain. "I found one."

He trotted over to her, and she held out the crystal. Even in the cold air, the crystal was warm when it touched his palm, the soul within strong enough to generate the heat. Or perhaps it was the spells binding the soul that created the warmth?

Not that it mattered. They had it now, and soon the soul would be taken to one of their temples where an elder would set it free.

"Can you tell if the soul is centaur or human?" he asked.

"Centaur," Seira confirmed after a moment's study. "Although I can't tell you a name or anything else about the soul. I have no way to communicate with it."

Toryn nodded and then reverently wrapped the soul crystal in a soft cloth before tucking it into one of his packs.

Seira stared at his pack for long moments. "It is

terrible to think of a noble soul locked away like that, helpless, trapped.

"But not forgotten. The soul is safe now. That is all that matters. Come, let us keep looking. There might be more bodies on this slope."

And he wasn't wrong. They soon stumbled upon another body. This one was as damaged as the first corpse. But there was good news. The mage had two soul crystals on him.

One was another centaur soul, and the other was a woman of the mountains. His breath froze in his lungs. He waited for Seira's magic to confirm if this was one of her sisters.

A few minutes later, a shake of her head told him it wasn't.

"I'm sorry," he said.

"As am I."

Once the two new soul crystals were safely tucked away in his pack, he and Seira returned to the ledge and looked out over the valley floor.

"Perhaps they're all dead? If they are, we can return with a larger force to retrieve the bodies and free the stolen souls," Toryn said. "If the bodies are unreachable, we'll return in the spring once the snow melts. I think the souls would understand the wait."

While Toryn had wanted to see the light fade out of

each soul-mage's gaze one by one, he knew it was better if they'd all died down there.

Though soul-mages had a reputation of surviving what would kill most other creatures. And as long as there was a chance some still lived, he couldn't turn back. They needed to see this through.

He glanced sidelong at Seira. "I can't believe we'd be so fortunate for them all to be dead. We'll need to go down there and see if there are any trails heading out of the avalanche area."

Seira frowned at the snow blocking the valley below them. "There is a way to find out that doesn't require us to go there."

He turned to study her silently. At last, she assuaged his curiosity.

"There is a triple alignment of the moons in three days. I will pray to my Goddess tonight to learn the fate of the soul-mages. And then during the alignment, I shall perform the spell of seeking. If some of the soul-mages escaped with the souls of our people, I'll be able to track their movements. Perhaps I'll even be able to call upon enough magic to wound the soul-mages from afar."

Toryn straightened to his full height. "I will lend you my magic as well. My tracking spells can aid you in your hunt."

"Thank you. I may need all the power you can spare."

He nodded. "Three days, then. We'll camp until it's time."

"I don't like waiting that long," she admitted and sighed. "But we don't have a choice."

"Even if some of the soul-mages survived the avalanche, they'll not be escaping these mountains anytime soon. And it will be safer for us if we don't have to cross the valley floor. There is still a substantial snowpack. Some of it might be unstable." Toryn nodded to the western slope. "One of my brothers used to have a patrol near here. I'm somewhat familiar with the area. There's a cave close by, higher up the slope. We'll gather some firewood and use that to shelter for the night."

"And what if there is a bear or other large predator already denning there?" Seira sounded tired.

Though he wasn't sure if that was exhaustion or emotional stress.

He gave his ax a swing and grinned, hoping to cheer her. "More meat for us. And if it's a bear, all the better. Their hides are very warm."

CHAPTER TWENTY-FIVE

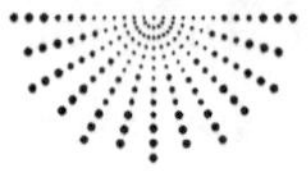

Seira

True to his word, Toryn was vaguely familiar with the area and was able to locate the cave with a little searching. It was extensive, with a reasonably flat floor. As far as shelters went, it was a good place to spend the next three days while they waited for the moons to align. The centaur used a large evergreen bough to sweep debris out of the cave while Seira unpacked their supplies.

She immediately noticed one of her pack's ties wasn't properly securing the flap of her bag in place. Jerking it open more, she saw an accumulation of snow inside. Likely from the times she'd ducked under low hanging branches as the centaur trotted in pursuit of the enemy.

"Curse it."

"What's wrong?" he asked as he paused in his work to peer over at her.

"I stupidly left my pack open. Some snow got inside."

He rubbed at his jaw, a smirk on his face. "I'd offer you something to wear while your clothing dries, but I'm too self-serving. I'd much rather you sit naked next to the fire while your garments dry."

Seira snorted as she began going through her things. "You seem to forget the clothing I'm wearing is dry. I'll be keeping that on until my other supplies are as well."

It wasn't until she started to notice green stains on the garments at the bottom that she realized her mistake in leaving the flap unsecured was going to be more than an inconvenience.

She pulled out the first full packet of her fertility suppression tea and found the powder had dissolved and soaked into the rest of her items.

Tearing other items out of her bag in rapid succession, she soon found the rest. The powder in the three-quarters-empty sac she'd been using from was dry, protected where it had slid between folds of a blanket. But the second full packet was just as wet as the first.

"Why didn't I think to double-check the buckle?" Seira breathed as she gazed at her green-stained fingers and clothing.

There wasn't enough of the dried powder to last a week. And once it was wet, it lost its potency quickly, rendering it useless. There would never be enough to finish the mission and get back home before she ran out.

Her hands shook with that realization. Going off the tea too suddenly could turn even the most sensible of women into fools. She couldn't allow herself to get that distracted. And distraction meant death when one was hunting soul-mages.

A large hand came to rest upon hers. "Easy, Priestess. I will not take advantage You have my word."

She snorted. "But I might take advantage of you, Centaur."

A red flush told her she'd surprised him, but his expression remained gentle as he placed his other hand over hers. "And no doubt, I'd normally enjoy such a thing under ideal conditions, but I have given you my word that I won't let anything happen while you are not yourself."

"Thank you." Though she trusted his word and knew he meant the words wholeheartedly now, that didn't mean his willpower would hold up if she became determined enough.

And she wouldn't lie to herself.

Even with the tea regulating her responses to him, she'd been drawn to the centaur this whole time. He was kind and gentle and trustworthy. But also a fierce and skilled warrior and hunter.

And while she was on a truth-telling tangent, she'd admit there had even been some thoughts on how she might convince him to return home with her. If the matrons were going to attempt to match her to a male, she'd prefer it to be Toryn.

Giving up the life she loved for the right male might not be such a hardship. And she was beginning to think more and more that Toryn was the right male for her.

"Do you have enough to wean yourself off the drug?"

His deep voice startled her out of her inappropriate thoughts.

She glanced up at him in surprise. "Wean myself off?"

"Yes. I'm no healer, but I've heard stories of centaurs being grievously injured in battle or a hunt gone bad and then having to endure months of healing. Some grow dependent on the herbs that dull pain, and the poor sods have to enter into another battle of sorts to gain their freedom from that dependence. The healers gradually lower their daily dosage of the pain relievers until the centaur in question can function without them."

Seira gave the bag that had been untouched by dampness a little shake, looking thoughtful. "I might not have enough to wean myself off as gently as a healer would, but it'll be better than suddenly going off it."

"I agree." He placed one hand on her shoulder. "And your will is strong. You will master this like any other enemy."

Seira nodded. "I'll be victorious in this as well."

CHAPTER TWENTY-SIX

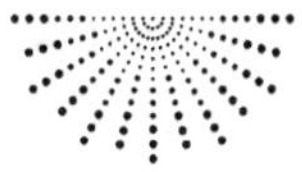

Seira

While she wouldn't be able to do any vast workings of magic like what would be needed to kill the group of soul-mages in one swift wave until the moons were in alignment, that didn't mean she couldn't get started now.

As soon as she knew Toryn didn't need her help with anything, she went outside and began to set up her small altar near the cave entrance.

Directly in front of her, a small candle served as a heat source to carry her prayer up into the heavens. To her left, a bowl of water sat, positioned perfectly to capture and reflect the Maiden's Moon on its mirror-like surface.

On her right side, she'd laid out a lit bundle of moonflower. Fire released its sweet fragrance. Soon it mixed with the more potent aroma of white sage.

Sitting cross-legged, she closed her eyes and began a soft chant, praising her deity for her protection and the gift of a warrior-priestess's magic. Once that was done, she shifted her thoughts to her dead sisters, beseeching her goddess to show her where their souls now resided.

Nothing happened at first, but then whirls of color appeared behind her closed eyelids. It was a field of white broken up by a bit of blue here and a dash of green there. Slowly a vision of a snow-covered mountain slope took form. A few coniferous trees still dotted the slope where the avalanche had failed to rip them from the ground.

Thick snow was falling in the vision, suggesting the location was somewhere deeper in the mountains. Soon her incorporeal form was flying along the valley floor as it began to climb higher up into the mountains.

In the way of visions, she had no control over the speed with which events unfolded. All she could do was wait and hope her goddess revealed what Seira needed to know and that she'd understand the meaning when she saw it.

But soon her rapid flight slowed, and she realized this vision wasn't going to be one of the ones that required a great deal of deliberation to understand. This one was clear.

A narrow trail cut through the deep snow showed the path the soul-mages had taken. Soon she was able to spot them midway up the slope. They were taking that route because the snow there was more stable, the loose accumulation having already made its hurried journey to the bottom of the slope in the earlier avalanche.

She continued to arrow toward the line of enemies making their slow and painful way along the slope. A headcount confirmed seventeen had survived of the original number. She had no way of knowing how many had died in the avalanche, but those males and females weren't her concern. Any soul-crystals trapped beneath the snow could be rescued later.

The greater concern was stopping the living soul-mages from escaping with their ill-got bounty. With her ethereal vision, she could see the glowing crystals hanging from their chains hidden under layers of cloaks and armor and fur-lined vests worn by the soul-mages.

But thanks to an earlier winter storm in the mountains, these living soul-mages would not make a swift escape as they had hoped. Perhaps they wouldn't escape at all.

It was still possible the mountains might claim the soul-mages. But she didn't plan to leave it to chance. She would hunt down each and every last one of the soul-stealing monsters and bury her blade in their hearts. Then she'd watch as their souls faded from their eyes.

If such a monstrous creature as a soul-mage actually still possessed a soul. She wasn't at all confident they did. Perhaps they bartered their own away to some dark god, and that was why they stole others.

But she didn't care about their reasoning. She'd still hunt down and kill them to the last man. She might even share a few of the kills with Toryn.

As she exhaled, Seira tapped her index finger against her opposite wrist four times, and the vision faded. When there was once again nothing but blackness behind her closed lids, she opened them.

In the vision's place, Toryn knelt before her, his legs folded under him in the snow.

"I thought you hated the snow?" she asked him.

"I do. What did you learn?"

There was no doubt in his eyes. He'd believed her when she'd said she could speak with her goddess. Perhaps Toryn had his own ways of communicating with his gods.

"We were wrong." She paused and sighed. "Some of them survived. Seventeen by my count. And they are still in possession of our peoples' souls." She snuffed out the candle and then ground the two herb bundles into their own ashes until the tiny bits of glowing embers faded. Lastly, she emptied the water from the bowl to her right and then stacked the others together. "They are still struggling through the deepening snow. But even a centaur can't catch them now, not with the mess the avalanche made of the valley."

Toryn climbed to his feet and then reached down to give her a hand up. "If we cannot kill them in person, we will kill them from afar."

Seira felt her one brow arch in question. "If that was possible, why haven't you tried it before now?"

"Because it wasn't possible before now. But after seeing the avalanche, it gave me an idea. You know centaurs are strong in earth and water magic. It's tied into our goddess-given gifts of tracking, speed, and stamina. We draw our power from the earth we walk upon."

He paused to let her assimilate that before continuing. "But we can also draw magic from one part of the land and send it into another location. It's how we can summon water from dry ground. We call it up by forcing magic down deep into the earth to displace the water, forcing it to the surface. If I managed to destabilize the foundation under the largest snowpack, I think I might be able to trigger more avalanches to complete our mission for us."

Hope bloomed in her heart.

Acting on a strange instinct she didn't fully understand—but she thought it might still have been the touch of her goddess acting upon her—she closed her other hand around the one Toryn was still gripping from helping her stand. Then she raised it to her lips. She placed a kiss to his knuckles and then turned his hand over and nudged his fingers open. Once the fingers were relaxed, she pressed her lips against his palm.

"May the Moon Goddess, the Mother of the Prairies, and the Lord of the Forest bless these hands so they can carry out divine will," she mumbled against his warm skin before placing a second—unneeded—kiss on his palm. Then acting under the influence of some devilish spirit, she flicked her tongue out and caressed the line that formed a crescent around the thicker flesh surrounding his thumb.

The centaur jerked at the touch, a shiver racing all the way down his body to the tip of his tail. When she looked up at his face, his eyes were wide, pupils dilated, lips parted in surprise, and his soft equine ears had emerged from his hair. Even they quivered ever so slightly.

"I see I finally managed to surprise you, Centaur."

His body relaxed in the next moments, and his infectious smile was back in place. "It happens to even the best of us. Now I'll have to see if I can raise a similar response in you when you least expect it."

Seira knew at that moment she'd started something that likely wasn't wise, and yet she couldn't help but laugh. "I look forward to seeing your disappointment when you fail."

He merely grinned harder, the light of mischief dancing in his eyes.

She smiled back but joy failed to touch her heart.

In three days, when the moons were in proper alignment, she and Toryn would, at last, have their vengeance. And then their mission would be over, and they would part ways. That thought made her deeply unhappy.

CHAPTER TWENTY-SEVEN

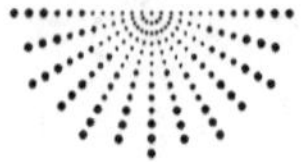

Seira

Once their cave was set up, dinner cooking over a central fire, her clothing laid out to dry and their shared bed arranged beside the fire, Seira fidgeted, not knowing what to do with herself as she waited for their meal to cook.

Usually, this was when she'd be making herself a cup of hormone controlling tea to sip at until their meat was done. But she'd decided to hold off and do a weak cup before bed instead. Then she'd skip it the next day, saving it for the morning after.

Looking for something else to do, she turned to

watch Toryn groom himself. He hadn't had a lot of free time to do so during their journey, and he was looking a little bedraggled.

She probably was as well.

With her lips twisting in humor, she rocked forward onto her toes. "Would you like some help grooming?"

He gave her a suspicious little look, as if not trusting her motives. "I would love to have your aid. However, I'm not sure if this is you or your newly awakening hormones wanting to groom me. Perhaps you should have your tea first?"

"I had the full dose last night at dinner. Even if I missed a day, its lack wouldn't affect me that fast." She rolled her eyes at him. "Besides, even if I went without for a moon cycle, I still wouldn't be interested in your great big horse's ass."

Toryn made such a funny dejected face she couldn't help laughing. Soon her merriment had him hooting his own mirth. Then while he was still chuckling, she started digging around in his pack until she found a couple of his grooming brushes and a hoof pick.

"Found them!" When she advanced, he retreated in a playful manner. Soon she was chasing him all over the cave while he played hard to catch, kicking up his heels and darting away while his tail flagged behind him.

When she got tired of chasing him, she stopped and gave him a pretend glower.

"Well, fine. Stay a muddy mess from the snowmelt. But there is no way I'm letting you near the blankets like that. Bad enough everything smells like centaur." Actually, she loved his scent. It was ten times more pleasant than anything she'd ever smelled in her life. "And I don't need my only dry clothing getting damp from you."

Though, he really wasn't that wet. A quick rubdown would remove most of the dampness.

As if her words were a threat or a command, he wheeled around and came prancing up to her. She had to rub at her nose to hide her smirk.

"I was only playing," he said in a rush. "I would love a good grooming. It has been ages since I've had another pair of hands to help."

Smiling, she grabbed the bit of cloth he used as a rubdown towel and tossed it over his back.

"When I'm done, you will be groomed until you gleam."

His lower body hadn't yet grown in his winter coat, but it was starting to show in the hints of a darker coloration in places. By late fall, he would turn from the pale gold of his summer coat to the darker, richer palomino she favored in that coloration.

Briefly, she wondered if the Moon Goddess saw fit

to match Seira with a centaur of her favorite color or if palomino had become her favorite color sometime over the last seven years.

When she thought back on it, she couldn't remember when she'd first decided palomino was her favorite color. But over the years, she'd started to look for pack horses in that coloration to carry her belongings when she traveled from the fortress city in the springtime. Not that color was more important than temperament, but most of the mountain horses were good-natured and well-trained.

As she worked to dry Toryn, she admitted he might have been the first palomino to capture her attention, and that interest had never faded. Instead, it had grown.

Now she couldn't imagine not having him near, even if it was across a river.

Not that she would ever tell Toryn that. It would blow his ego out of proportion. The last thing she needed was him strutting and prancing and flagging his tail around her any more than he already was.

As promised, she groomed him until he gleamed.

Then both feeling relaxed and pleased with the trust they'd built, they ate their meal in silence. Afterward, exhausted from a long day, they climbed into their shared bedding.

As usual, when he was in centaur form, she took the

section next to the wall, and he rested on his side at the edge of the pallet with his four legs pointed toward the fire while the rest of him was under the blanket.

Briefly, Seira noted the cave was warm enough with a fire burning that they didn't actually need to sleep together, but Toryn seemed very fond of sharing body heat. And she was very fond of his scent.

She'd often wake to find herself snuggled up to his back, her arms wrapped around his human waist. Neither of them ever said anything. Seira was too embarrassed that she'd strayed to his side in the night, and she was confident he held his silence because he knew he'd find himself sleeping alone if he said anything.

Their sleeping arrangement suited her just fine as long as he continued to behave.

CHAPTER TWENTY-EIGHT

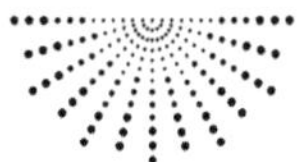

Toryn

He woke from a very heated dream only to wonder if he was still dreaming. Seira was cuddling next to him, her long calloused fingers stroking his skin in gentle circles. At first, he thought she was awake, but a glance at her face showed she was still asleep.

The knowledge only lessened the pleasure of her touch a little. Especially when she half rolled onto him and her one leg entwined with his, her smaller foot stroking along his very human ones.

Goddess, the dream had been so compelling, he'd

shifted to human form in his sleep, which should have been concerning, but he had other things demanding his attention.

When her hand drifted lower, his cock twitched, begging for her touch. If he hadn't given his word that he'd do nothing to attempt to seduce her, he might have given in to the temptation of feeling her fingers close around his needy flesh.

But he'd given his word.

And, great God of the Forest, he was regretting it now. His hips jerked up when her hand slid a bit farther before relaxing.

He slowly pushed the blankets down out of the way because if she kept touching him in her sleep, he was going to spill. Closing his eyes, he reached for his cock and recaptured the dream.

Only to freeze a few moments later when Seira snuggled closer, a wandering hand moving in gentle circles as if her petting was an attempt to calm him.

Groaning, he worked his hand up and down with more vigor. Close. He was close now, and with Seira's scent surrounding him and the warm weight of her breasts pressed against his side, this time was better than anything he'd ever experienced. Back bowed, hips thrusting up into the air, he dug his heels into the furs under him.

"Seira…" He envisioned her hands on him. "Hmm… so close."

He was on the precipice.

"What are you doing!"

He froze mid-thrust. But it wasn't her tone; it was the sharp edge of her blade that had him stopping so suddenly he might just have strained every muscle in his body.

She pressed the flat of her blade to his throat, and against all reason, his balls drew up even tighter. *I have an issue,* he decided.

"Explain." The single word was harsh, but her warm breath across his ear was so very sweet his hips gave an involuntary little thrust.

"Isn't it painfully obvious," he managed to gasp out while holding back his release. Now, while she had a lethal little blade pressed to his throat, wasn't the time to startle the uptight warrior-priestess. "Stress the painful part."

He swallowed and felt a slight sting and a wet warmth against his skin.

"Easy," he whispered. "I wasn't going to touch you. I just woke up from a dream, and you were pressed against me. I couldn't stop myself."

She eased the blade away from his neck and looked down at herself. "I'm fully dressed."

"Aren't you always?"

She glowered at him. "I meant you didn't try to undress me."

"No. I gave you my word. I'll never break it. Especially not to you, the woman I…"

One of her thumbs suddenly brushed his lower lip. He closed his eyes and gritted his teeth as his hips gave another jerk.

But to his surprise, he felt her relax back against him, and she sheathed the knife.

He blinked at her stupidly. "You're not going to geld me?"

She grinned. "No. You didn't touch me, and I have no right to dictate what you do with yourself."

He noted her gaze was no longer on his face. His eager cock seemed to have realized the same thing and gave a hopeful little twitch. He tightened his death grip around it as if he could strangle it into submission.

That never worked, though.

"Looks…painful," she murmured. There was a look of fascination on her face when she spoke the words.

He only then realized he was missing an opportunity to show her what he could bring to a relationship.

"A little."

She propped her head on her hand and looked down at him for a time.

"I've never seen a male… like this. I'm curious." She looked back at his face a moment later, and then she surprised him to the bottom of his soul. "Is it inappropriate to ask to watch you finish?"

"No," he said as he fought back a groan. He sensed she was at the end of her nerve. If he did something stupid, she'd bolt. And he very much wanted her to stay.

He ordered his body to calm even as he gave himself a firm stroke. He wanted to last long enough to give her something to watch, but it was a battle to hold back the end.

Then she surprised the heck out of him a second time and ran her thumb across his mushroom-shaped head, spreading the wetness over his hot skin. He hissed, his back arching as he fought to hold back.

"Goddess! Seira, do that again."

She hesitated for a moment. But then she closed her fingers over him and caressed him awkwardly. And as swiftly as the caress of her fingers closed around him, it was all over, his seed erupting out of him for so long and so fiercely he should probably have been embarrassed, but all he felt was joy that she'd finally touched him.

His joy evaporated in the next moment as she leaped up and stepped over his naked body without so much as acknowledging what her gentle, inquisitive touch had done to him. Goddess, he was still panting and twitching. Where was she going? He wanted to hold her, to feel her warmth next to him.

Moving over to the fire, she began to build it up. Then she looked toward their dwindling supply of firewood.

"We need more fuel for the fire if we're going to be stuck here for another day or two. When you're dressed, go collect some for the fire. I'll go hunting before the snow gets any deeper."

With that, she busied herself fussing with her bow and quiver in an effort to ignore him and what they'd just done. Or perhaps she was trying to ignore what she'd done to him and how it made her feel.

Because he was damned sure she felt a considerable lot of something. Otherwise, she wouldn't have jumped up and away like he was on fire.

CHAPTER TWENTY-NINE

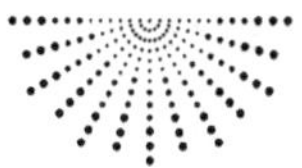

Toryn

Grumpy that he had to go out into the cold when all he really wanted to do was roll over and go back to sleep with Seira tucked against his side, he pulled on his boots—by the goddess, he hated boots—and stomped out into the snow. In the warm weather, he preferred to go barefoot, but in this ice and snow and slush, he didn't have a choice.

Scanning the terrain, he decided to go farther down the slope to gather fallen wood, leaving what was closer to the cave's entrance for later in case the weather turned worse and traveling even a short distance became difficult.

Even as he gathered wood, he instinctively kept an eye on Seira's progress down the slope until she disappeared in denser shrubbery. Sighing wistfully that he couldn't watch her graceful progress, he returned his attention to the task at hand.

He gathered wood until midday.

At least he thought it was midday. It was impossible to see the sun's position behind the thick grey clouds that blanketed the mountains. More snow was already falling, thick and fluffy, promising to hide whatever tracks he left.

Not that he was concerned about anyone following them into the mountains. The need would be dire to send someone hunting after them into this frozen land.

He and Seira certainly wouldn't have been here if duty and honor hadn't set them on this path.

As he ducked under a low hanging bough, a branch's worth of snow fell upon his head, and some of it inevitably trickled down his back. Snarling, he shook the snow out of his hair and continued back to the cave, taking large strides and leaping up the slope.

This was going to be his last load of wood for the day. If they burned through this, he'd collect more tomorrow.

He leaped over the loose patch of shale and gravel just below the cave entrance but miscalculated his leap, forgetting for a moment that he didn't have the jumping power he had in his centaur form.

His leading foot landed in the loose ground. It slipped. Tossing aside his armload of wood, he attempted to grab at the shrubby growth that had taken root in the solid ground to his immediate right, but his leap fell short, and he landed on his belly as the loose stone shifted under him and began to slip downslope.

Clawing at the loose stone, he fought to find some kind of handholds, but the substrate was too deep for him to find a solid surface underneath.

Twisting his body, he flipped over and drew his ax, trying to snag anything that would slow his rapid descent. But nothing worked.

As he continued to speed toward the edge of the cliff, he roared his rage and denial, but it did nothing to stop him from shooting over the side.

CHAPTER THIRTY

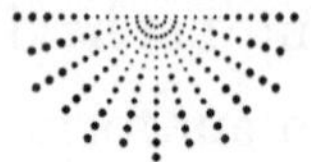

Seira

Toryn wasn't in the cave, and she hadn't seen him on the slope as she was returning with her kill. Equally as concerning was that the cave was cold, the fire having gone out. Toryn hated the cold. He wouldn't have let the fire go out. It took too long for the cave to warm up once more.

There were several piles of wood stacked in one corner of the cave that hadn't been there before. Clearly, Toryn had been back several times while she'd been out hunting.

But where was he now?

Had something happened?

Could they have been mistaken and there was a living soul-mage around here somewhere, and she hadn't found him?

No. That was unlikely. She'd located all the others, even the dead.

Glancing out the uncovered cave entrance at the heavily falling snow, she decided it was much more likely he'd gotten lost in the poor visibility, or he'd fallen and injured himself.

She hurried out of the cave, already scanning the ground for lumps and bulges under the snow that she didn't remember having been there before. Carefully avoiding the treacherous section of loose shale and rubble now hidden under the snow, she made her way downslope.

It was by accident that she stepped on a piece of wood and discovered more scattered around. There was too much to have fallen naturally in this one spot. Using her boot, she kicked away snow, looking for more evidence of what had happened to the centaur.

Partway down the slope, she found a scrap of his shirt. She snatched it up and ran her fingers over it as if it could tell her where its owner was. Of course, she couldn't learn anything from the fabric except that Toryn had been this way. The state of the fabric suggested he'd rapidly come down the slope, and it hadn't been under his own power.

She continued down, her eyes scanning for more evidence or lumps in the snow. But there was nothing except the steep grade and then open sky.

With a heavy heart, she carefully made her way to the edge and peered over. She half expected to see his broken body at the bottom of the cliff, if she saw anything at all.

What she hadn't expected was a ledge an arm's length below the edge, and upon it was an unconscious, snow-covered Toryn.

She leaned down and felt around until she found his pulse. He was alive. Sobbing in relief, she thanked the goddess.

Eyeing the ledge, and uncertain how stable it was, she decided it was safer to grab him by the arms and haul him back up onto the slope where she knelt.

The task was easier to complete in her mind than in reality.

He weighed a lot, but she managed to drag him up. Once there, she pulled him farther from the edge and then swiftly checked him over. As far as she could tell under his clothing, he didn't have any broken bones, but the back of his head had a large bump and blood wet his scalp.

She worried over that, but there was nothing she could do for it out here, so she heaved him up over her shoulder and began to climb back up to the top.

Half-way up she fell, and they both ended up sprawled on the snow-covered ground. Then with a whispered apology and a mighty heave, she lifted him back up and continued her trek.

At last, the cave came into sight. She nearly sobbed in relief, and she realized how great a blessing it was that he was in the shape of a man this morning and not his centaur form. If he'd been half equine, she never would have been able to move him.

Soon she stumbled into the cave and walked over to their sleeping pallet where she deposited him there as gently as possible. Then she rushed over to the fire and began building it.

Toryn was too cold. The first order of business was getting the cave warm and then seeing to his injuries.

CHAPTER THIRTY-ONE

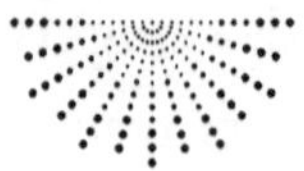

Seira

After the fire was roaring, she carefully checked his head wound. She was grateful the skin was just torn. His skull felt intact under the skin. Though he had a bloody big welt on his head and he'd likely have the mother of all headaches when he woke.

"You have to wake up," she whispered to him. "You're too stubborn to die. And I don't know what I'd do without you, you great stubborn horse's ass."

For a time, she had trouble seeing what she was doing, her vision blurred by her tears. But as she focused on her work, her tears dried. After removing his clothing, she carefully washed and bandaged any cuts and scrapes she discovered.

There wasn't actually that much damage. His leather clothing had protected him from the majority of the harm. She was just worried about his head. But when she lifted his eyelids, both pupils reacted to the light from her candle. Neither was sluggish. That was a good sign. Her mentors had taught her that much.

If Seira had been farther into her healer studies, she might have attempted to call upon that magic to tend his head wound, but she also remembered her mentors saying head injuries were complicated and sometimes it was better just to let them heal naturally or wait until a more skilled healer could arrive.

But no help was coming.

Seira decided to wait and see if he would recover on his own. If it looked like he was getting worse, she would try her hand at healing his head wound.

Studying him for a time, she tilted her head and then stroked a hand down his chest.

"Don't die on me, horseman. I don't know what I'd do without you to make my life interesting."

With all his wounds tended to and nothing else needing her immediate attention, she crawled in bed next to Toryn and tucked herself against his side.

CHAPTER THIRTY-TWO

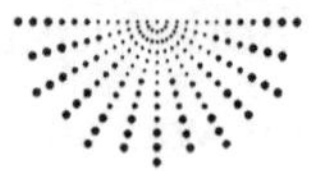

Toryn

A good half of his body ached. He thought about going back to sleep, not really wanting to know what catastrophe had befallen him this time to make him hurt so much. Damn. It really did feel like half his body was a bruise.

But then a warm body snuggled against him, and he realized he wasn't alone. Suddenly waking up had a much greater appeal. Grunting softly as his muscles twitched in warning, he opened his eyes as he turned to the source of the warmth.

Seira.

His favorite warrior-priestess was holding him, her body pressed up against his.

He blinked a moment later in confusion. He was naked.

How had he come to be sleeping naked with Seira?

As much as he hated clothing, she always made him get dressed before he climbed in bed with her if he was human. He didn't know what had occurred to soften Seira toward his preferences, but he liked it and wanted to discover how to replicate the miracle.

When his mind still came up with nothing, he just pressed his face against her neck and breathed in her calming scent. Soon his hands were roaming over her body, caressing her curves through her clothing.

He probably should stop. Hadn't he given her his word that he would never take advantage of her?

Huffing in annoyance, he leaned back and then grunted in surprise when he saw her eyes were open. She blinked sleepily at him a couple times. But instead of growling and snarling and demanding to know why he was naked, she returned his caresses instead, her fingers seeking out his skin.

Soon she was kissing him and whispering soft, seductive words into his ears.

This delightful turn of events had him returning her eager caresses until he remembered that he'd given her his promise that he wouldn't do anything to compromise her magic while they were still on their mission.

Damnation.

"Seira," he groaned as she stroked him. "We should stop. Your tea."

She lifted her head and gazed down at him with the most open and loving look he'd ever received.

"You came so close to death," she whispered in a broken sob. "I came so close to losing you. If I'd taken any longer on the hunt, you might have died before I found you." Her voice broke. "The Moon Goddess grants her priestess's many gifts. But the power to heal death isn't one of them."

"I…what happened?" But even as he asked, memories of what had occurred came back to him, his miscalculation and fall, sliding down the slope, and then over the edge.

"Make love to me." Seira leaned down then and kissed him, her lips soft and demanding.

"I-I can't," Toryn stuttered as he turned away, breaking her kiss.

When she pulled away, her expression didn't show hurt, though.

"Of course. You're still too weak from your ordeal." She lowered her lips back to his. "Allow me to make love to you then, my fierce centaur."

Oh Goddess, please smite whatever spirit of mischief is having fun at my expense.

"Lovely, lovely Seira. We can't," he said, taking hold of her shoulders. "Your tea."

"I don't care about that."

"I do. I gave you my word."

She dropped her head against his chest. After a moment, she started to laugh. "I never thought you'd be the one saying no."

And you have no idea how much it pains me.

She lifted her head and looked him in the eyes. "You're going to stay there and recover, and I'm going to attend to every one of your other needs that you'll allow me to attend."

"You'll get no fight from me," he said with a grin, and then added, "As long as we continue with our original plan. I'm not so hurt that I can't do my part. And if we don't act while the moons are aligned, we won't have another chance to destroy the soul-mages for another month."

She nodded. "Tomorrow we destroy the last of the soul-mages foolish enough to venture upon our lands."

CHAPTER THIRTY-THREE

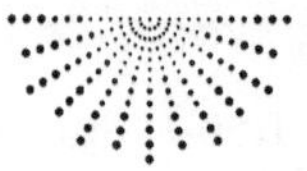

Seira

Standing shoulder to shoulder with the centaur, Seira gazed upon the small altar they'd built for this task. Upon it sat the bowl, candle, sage, and moonflower. And beside those symbols of the Moon Goddess sat a braid of sweet-smelling grass Toryn had woven.

Next to the grass sat the two wooden statues he'd carved for her. Last in line was a small acorn. The grass represented the goddess of the prairies, and the acorn was one taken from the centaur god's sacred forest.

Toryn had explained that all centaurs carried a few of the sacred acorns.

With these simple objects, they hoped to summon the aid of all three deities and command enough power to destroy the remaining soul-mages.

There was no guarantee. The mages had continued to travel to the south and were making better time than Seira had hoped. They might already be beyond her reach.

But she and Toryn could only try. They would not give up, not as long as the soul-mages still breathed.

Seira began the ritual, singing softly of her Goddess's power and might and sense of justice. Toryn joined in, beseeching his divine prairie mother to aid them in their hunt for these enemies. Then Toryn called to the Forest Lord.

Each time they called to the divine, more power danced above the altar.

Their gods were with them.

Together they repeated the ritual words of summoning three more times. Once the sacred number was reached, the three powers combined upon the altar, swirling and dancing in the air, an ethereal fire whipped up by an unseen hand.

Then between one moment and the next, the three magics separated, and those differently hued powers rushed toward them. The brighter, silver-blue magic of the Moon Goddess flowed into Seira, its warmth working deeper into her body and mind.

While it was stronger than any flow she'd called upon in the past, it was still familiar, and she welcomed it like an old friend. In the same moment, the sky-blue power of the prairie goddess and the deep green magic of the Forest Lord flowed into Toryn until the centaur was glowing with power.

She glanced down at herself to find she was outlined in a similar soft glow.

Turning to look back up at Toryn, she gave him a fierce smile. "Now the soul-mages will pay for their treachery."

Toryn nodded and reached out a hand. She took it. Once again, the three powers joined, this time through their bodies. Closing her eyes, she could feel the powers, both foreign and familiar. Her centaur partner pushed a little more of the power toward her, allowing her to take the lead.

She accepted it willingly, and then in her mind's eye, she looked out beyond the opening of their cave to the mountains beyond. Back in her physical body, she felt his fingers squeeze hers and then suddenly his mind was flying through the storm next to her.

Briefly, she debated calling on the storm to follow

them, but storms, even the fastest among them, were too slow to keep up with her and Toryn as they flew through the skies.

Somewhere ahead, the trapped souls of her people called to her, and she raced in pursuit, Toryn's spirit still at her side. She did not know how long they flew.

Time was not the same to a soul set free from its body. Beside her, Toryn's essence touched her.

"I can feel the soul-mages. My tracking gift is much stronger, boosted by the gods. We are close. Be ready," he warned. His body was back in the cave and yet she could still hear his words. "We don't know if they can sense us or not."

"I understand," she said, turning her attention back to the task at hand.

Then continuing to move with incredible speed, they quickly overtook the group of soul-mages. Seira eyed the group of seventeen cloak-shrouded figures. She noticed they were no longer on horseback.

"They've ridden their horses to death," Toryn said, a hint of disdain thick in his tone.

"Or the beasts were killed in that earlier avalanche. Either way, it makes me feel that much less guilty about dropping a mountainside down upon them if I'm not killing some innocent horses at the same time."

Toryn nodded, and then he was sharing power with

her again. "Take as much as you need to create the avalanche."

Seira nodded even though she wasn't in her body. Then reaching deep, she dipped her hands into the wellspring of power gifted to her by the gods.

The power flared, rising to her will, and soon it was darting through the air. Tendrils of burning light and mist, a swirling vortex of energy erupted out of the air all around her.

Moments before the power struck the mountainside, she directed it to fork like lightning. At her command, the power lanced out and targeted different regions of the snowpack all along the northern slope of the mountain.

After the traces of magic in the air faded, there was silence. But below the still pristine surface of the snow, she could feel the magic working. She waited and watched. Patient. Serene.

And then the first sheet of snow high up on the peak gave way. Soon it triggered other sections. A low rumble swelled, growing deeper and louder.

In the valley floor below where she and Toryn's spirits floated, the soul-mages looked up at the collapsing snowpack. But within moments, the cloak-covered figures were calling on their own magic.

"They're trying to protect themselves." Eyes narrowing, Seira again scanned the wall of snow rushing toward the cloaked figures. "It won't do them any good. Even if they survive the first great blow, they'll be trapped. Once they exhaust their magic stores, their protective shield spells will fail. The weight of the snow will crush them."

"I'm not sure if that…" Toryn shifted suddenly, racing toward her. "Move!"

Toryn's spirit collided with her, and suddenly they were both tumbling toward the southern slopes of the mountain.

A moment later, a lance of oily black magic that reminded her of tar—if tar could take on a harden substance like a shard of glass—speared through the area she'd just been.

Even over the distance, she could feel the cold burn of power. "Goddess! I wasn't aware they could even see us."

"Now we know." Toryn's dry reply had the corner of her mouth twitching with humor. Did nothing phase the centaur?

Keeping her attention on the valley floor as more snow continued to avalanche down from higher up, she reached out for Toryn. Then their fingers closed around each other in spirit form.

Together they waited in silence until the snows no

longer cascaded down from above. Shortly afterward, the slopes were still once more. No movement beyond the sway of the few trees not ripped from the ground.

"I don't like leaving the soul-crystals down there with those monsters." She frowned unhappily, and then added, "The mages might feed upon the souls to strengthen their own magic a little longer."

Toryn galloped a circle around her in the sky, his tail a banner behind him. "I might have a way to rescue the soul-crystals that doesn't involve waiting for the spring melt."

His tone suggested he already had something planned. She turned toward him with an arched brow. "Speak, Horseman."

Tilting his head, he indicated the snow-covered valley below them. "When my tracking gift first detected the soul-mages, I noticed the soul-crystals reverberated softly to the touch of my magic. I think I may be able to call them up from the snow like I can call water up from the ground."

"Try it. But be careful of traps," she warned.

Seira watched in fascination as magic began swirling around Toryn's spirit. Otherwise, he remained unmoving. If Seira had used only visual cues, she'd have assumed nothing was happening. But something *was* happening deep down below the surface of the snow.

A moment later, a small glowing crystal erupted up out of the icy surface. A heartbeat later, another three appeared with little geysers of flakes. Soon more and more of them were breaking the crush to fly toward Toryn.

"It worked," Seira breathed, the last of the tension between her shoulder blades finally melting away.

Toryn looked as in awe as she felt. A moment later, he shook off his surprise and disbelief and opened his arms wide. The small star-like bits of pure light streaked toward him like he was a mother duck and they were his little ones seeking shelter under his wings.

Once the three dozen soul-crystals were hovering close to Toryn, he turned and tugged upon Seira's hand, and together they led their strange flying herd back to the cave.

CHAPTER THIRTY-FOUR

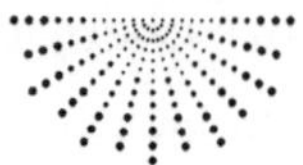

Seira

Holding the two soul-crystals up to the sun, she smiled sadly at them. The relief at having rescued them was immense, but now grief waited at the edge of her mind, ready to prey upon her at the first hint of weakness.

"You will be back at Blackstone soon. And then you will be free. I am only sorry I wasn't there to help you fight them." Sighing softly, she blinked back tears and then gently tucked the two crystals under her shirt and vest.

It wasn't that she didn't trust Toryn to carry them with the rest of the soul-crystals in the pack. She just wasn't ready to part with them again so soon after their rescue.

Now that the mission was almost over, another thought entered her mind and would not leave.

As one of the last breeding age females of her line, she knew she would be required to beget children almost as soon as she returned home. The thought left her feeling hollow inside.

But there was one male who made her happy.

She turned to Toryn suddenly. He was leaning down, packing the rest of their supplies.

"Father my children."

Toryn straightened so fast he nearly sat on his haunches. Only his sharp centaur reflexes and some excellent hoof work saved him from sitting on his ass.

"I don't want a slave mate. I want a partner," she continued doggedly before she lost her nerve. "I want you. And I don't want to share you."

"Seira." The one word was so full of longing, she found herself moving to his side.

"I'll birth as many children as I safely can to appease both our peoples."

"My beautiful priestess, are you certain? I want this

more than anything," he said in a rush and then paused, before continuing more slowly. "But it will not be easy. We'll be defying both our peoples."

"Nothing wonderful is ever easy. I want this. I want you." She stepped closer and then tilted her chin up. "And I'm willing to fight for what I want."

Toryn grinned like an idiot and dipped his head for a kiss.

She blocked him. "You need to hear the rest of my plan."

He grunted but was more than willing to listen as she explained how they would live as a family, making their home along the river for three seasons of the year. And then in the winter, she would take her daughters to Blackstone to learn the ways of the mountains, and he would take his centaur sons to the warmer coastal wintering grounds of his people.

But for the other months of the year, she and Toryn would be free to live and love as they wished.

Toryn grinned. "I like the picture you paint, but what if I don't want to be parted from half my family for the bitter months? Is there any chance I can seduce my beautiful priestess to come winter in warmer climates?"

"I would say you should be happy for what we can manage." She reached up and pressed a kiss to his lips to take the sting out of her words. "But I know you can be very persuasive, Horseman."

Though his idea did have appeal. Regrettably, she also had a responsibility to her people. And there was still much she could learn from the matrons about healing magic.

It was an important skill to learn and one she'd want to teach her daughters when they were old enough.

Worry crossed his features. "But what if your matrons force-match you to another this winter while I'm far away and unable to help?"

She reached up and smoothed away his frown lines.

"I will tell them that I am willing to become a mother, but that I will only settle for the fastest and strongest of studs to father my children. That no barely-fertile male will paw at me in a feeble attempt to father a child."

Toryn grinned in delight. "You barely had a taste of me, and I've already ruined you for other males."

"You can just calm that attitude down, my cocky stud. But if you behave, I might just let you plant your seed before I return to my people for the long winter. If you are as virile as you claim, I won't have to worry about being force-mated to another if I'm already carrying your child in my belly." She stroked a calming hand down his chest when he shivered at her words. "And the matrons will be well pleased and might even see the benefit of currying favor with free males if they are more fertile."

"I'm very game to try." His smirk stretched across his face. "And we might even smooth the way for peace between our peoples. And if the soul-mages are again planning raids upon our lands, it is past time we resurrected the old alliances."

"We could start now," Seira said, a seductive note in her tone. And then she was moving into his arms.

He hoisted her up like she weighed nothing.

Toryn's lips were warm and firm against hers. She was just melting into him when he froze. A moment later, a pounding reached her ears. At first, she thought it was the rushing of her blood, then she thought it was another avalanche somewhere in the mountains, but then Toryn was jerking away from her. He spun to face the new threat.

A company of thirty heavily armed centaurs, their hooves crunching on the stone, skidded to a halt outside the entrance to the cave. They fanned out to block escape to either side.

"Toryn," Seira called softly so her voice wouldn't carry. "Are these males friends of yours?"

"Depends on how angry my father is at me for leaving my post. Heck if I know how he found out I was gone?"

A tall, heavily muscled beast of a centaur trotted up to them. "Toryn, you great idiot. Are you all right? We've been smelling hints of soul-mage since before your trail entered the mountains."

"I am fine. But I had a pressing issue that needed my attention more than guarding a bit of wilderness along a peaceful border." Toryn paced over to the saddlebag that had been carefully packed to protect the soul-crystals. He pulled two chains out and showed them to the assembled centaurs.

There was a low muttering and an uneasy shifting in the gathered centaurs.

"We hunted the mages down and saw to it that they were unable to harm another innocent," Toryn explained. "To the best of our knowledge, we were able to destroy all the soul-mages and rescue every one of the souls trapped in the crystals. We were just discussing what our next course of action would be after we delivered the souls of our people to our elders."

"In that case, I can help with your decision. Your father requires your attendance immediately at court. You can tell us your tale on the way back." The big centaur looked Seira up and down. "And I most certainly want to know this pretty filly's name and how you captured her."

Seira's gaze flicked to Toryn before sliding back to the big black centaur. She tightened her fingers around the hilt of her sword.

Toryn ignored the older centaur's words. "I'm due back within a moon cycle anyway. What's so important that it required an entire company to chase me down? I'm more than capable of taking care of my own concerns."

The big male's gaze glinted with a hard light. "Your older brother is dead."

One of Toryn's hind legs stomped in his shocked surprise.

Sweeping into a deep bow, the big black addressed the younger centaur again. "Crown Prince Vecidan is dead. Long live Crown Prince Toryn."

If a hole had opened in the ground beneath Seira's feet and swallowed her, she wouldn't have been more shocked by the news.

Her centaur huntsman was actually royalty.

And just like that, Seira's dream of living with Toryn, of being free and continuing to explore this new relationship and all its potential, died in a blink.

She took a half step away from his side. Then another and another until she'd put some distance between them.

Toryn was still so shocked by the news of his brother's death that he hadn't noticed her missing from his side, but just as she was taking another step, he looked in her direction.

His tense gaze noticed the distance she'd put between them. Pain flashed across his features before he smoothed his expression into a more neutral mask.

Her body swayed forward at that flash of pain, but he turned away, returning his attention to the older centaur. Seira rocked back on her heels and held her position.

"How?" he asked, a fresh wave of pain flooding his voice.

"A hunting accident. It was witnessed by your youngest brother."

"Accident?" The single word was said in a chilling tone that sent a shiver fingering its way down Seira's spine.

"He claims. A female of a noble family was with him at the time I'm told. The evidence does support that it was an accident."

Seira didn't know this male or his mannerisms, but

even she could read his skepticism. He didn't believe the death of Toryn's older brother was an accident.

And by Toryn's body language, he didn't either. "I'll return and discover the truth. If my brother was assassinated, I will kill the one responsible."

The older centaur bowed once more. "Good. Let's move. We dare not linger here. If there was one group of soul-mages, there could be more."

"We will escort Seira back to her lands first." Toryn's tone was harsh; it left no room for argument or discussion. Or at least, that's likely what he hoped.

Seira was equally as stubborn as him. Reaching down, she pressed her hand against the two soul-crystals resting between her breasts.

You both will forgive me if I complete one more mission before returning you to our elders, won't you? She asked the souls of her sisters.

While she had no way to communicate with them, both crystals warmed pleasantly before cooling again. She wasn't sure if that was a 'yes' or a 'no,' but it seemed positive, so she'd take it as a yes.

Turning her attention fully back to Toryn, she stepped closer and reached for his hand.

"You don't know me at all if you think I'm going to let you gallop into danger without me. I find I've grown attached to you, Horseman. I'm coming with you whether you want me to or not."

That beautiful boyish smile she loved so much graced his lips, and then he was reaching a hand toward her. "I would not have asked it of you."

"And I would not be much of a partner if I made you ask."

"Your support means much to me." His voice thickened with emotions, and he had to swallow it down before continuing. "It will be dangerous, and I shouldn't allow you to come at all, but it means a great deal to have you with me while I hunt for my brother's assassin. Seira of Blackstone, I thank you once more for your friendship."

The black-coated centaur's head jerked up at the name. He looked Seira up and down. "I should have known. Toryn has always had a taste for danger. Well, Seira of Blackstone, it's good to make your acquaintance. If you ever hurt my nephew, I'll kill you myself. Am I clear?"

"Uncle!" Toryn placed an arm around her shoulders, trying to drag her closer, but Seira resisted so she could face the older centaur.

"Good. As you should." She stood firm and studied Toryn's uncle. "Toryn and I are friends. I'll hunt and kill anyone who means him harm. And if it puts you at ease,

I'll give you my word. I'll never harm Toryn. Annoy him? Discipline him? Tell him 'no' until he's sick of hearing it? Yes to all that, but I'll never harm him."

"Good. We understand each other perfectly." Then the big male spun on his heels and issued orders for the others. "Divide up and help carry the prince's gear. He'll have enough of a load with his priestess."

"Seira." Toryn's tone was somber. "You don't have to come with me. I wasn't lying. It will be dangerous."

She snorted and then swung herself up onto his back. "I thrive on danger as much as you, in case you hadn't noticed. Besides, you're an even bigger idiot than I thought if you think I'll let you ride into danger without me."

"Goddess, I love your ferocity, woman. Have I told you your sharp tongue and fiery spirit stirs my blood something fierce?" Toryn asked with a laugh.

"Not in so many words, but you're not subtle. I figured it out on my own." She reached back and smacked him on his rump. "Now move. We have a new mission."

"The royal court isn't ready for you. Goddess, I can't wait to see their faces the first time you open your mouth."

No, the court of the centaurs wasn't ready for her,

and she'd show no mercy to anyone who meant Toryn harm.

No one threatened her Huntsman.

It didn't matter if he was the crown prince and the life she'd wanted with him was impossible, she'd still stay until the end of this new mission. Once she'd neutralize this new threat and the prince was safe, then she would return to her own people with the souls of her sisters.

She would not dream of more. Dreams were for other people. But she would ride with Toryn for a little while longer and enjoy the warmth of his humor and his boyish smiles and his sexy little blushes.

Then Toryn raced after his uncle, and Seira was clinging to his broad back. With a laugh of pure joy, she allowed herself to feel the elation of riding on the back of the centaur she loved.

THE END

Toryn and Seira's story continues in Night Huntress.

Click here to start reading.

Hey before you go, can I interest you in signing up for my author newsletter?
As a gift for joining, you get my Free Starter Library.

http://lisablackwood.com/join-the-newsletter-here/

DID YOU ENJOY MASTER OF THE HUNT?

If you have a moment and wouldn't mind leaving a review, that would be greatly appreciated.

Reviews help other readers to decide if a book is something they would like.
It doesn't need to be long. Even a few words is tremendously helpful.

I also have a Facebook Reader group you might like.

https://www.facebook.com/groups/615663822176120/

None of this would have been possible without, you, my readers.

You're awesome!

Thank You!

Lisa Blackwood

BOOKS BY LISA BLACKWOOD

Gargoyle & Sorceress

Dawn of the Sorceress

Sorceress Awakening

Sorceress Rising

Sorceress Hunting

Sorceress at War

Sorceress Enraged

Legacy of the Sorceress

Sorcery & Firedrakes

Scion of the Sorceress

Sorceress Eternal

In Deception's Shadow Series (Epic Fantasy Romance)

Betrayal's Price

Herd Mistress

Maiden's Wolf

Death's Queen

The Prince's Gryphon (forthcoming)

Ishtar's Legacy Series (Epic Fantasy Romance)

Ishtar's Blade

The Blade's Beginning (short story)

Blade's Honor

Blade's Destiny

The Blade's Shadow

First Queen of the Gryphons

The King of the Anunnaki (forthcoming)

The Anunnaki's Blade (forthcoming)

Huntress vs Huntsman (Epic Fantasy Romance)

Master of the Hunt

Night Huntress

Dragon Archer

Soul Mage (forthcoming)